The Friendship Feature

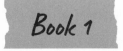

Book 1

THE

Jessie

FILES

A BOXCAR CHILDREN BOOK

The Friendship Feature

Book 1

Stacia Deutsch

Based on Characters Created by Gertrude Chandler Warner

Albert Whitman & Company
Chicago, Illinois

Library of Congress Cataloging-in-Publication data
is on file with the publisher.

Text copyright © 2022 by Albert Whitman & Company
First published in the United States of America in 2022
by Albert Whitman & Company
ISBN 978-0-8075-3786-2 (hardcover)
ISBN 978-0-8075-3787-9 (ebook)

THE BOXCAR CHILDREN® is a registered trademark
of Albert Whitman & Company.

Printed in the United States of America
10 9 8 7 6 5 4 3 2 1 LB 26 25 24 23 22 21

Jacket art copyright © 2022 by Albert Whitman & Company
Jacket art by Mina Price
Design by Aphelandra
Chapter opener graphic sourced from Vecteezy (@doraclub)

The Boxcar Children® created by Gertrude Chandler Warner

Visit The Boxcar Children® online at www.boxcarchildren.com.
For more information about Albert Whitman & Company,
visit our website at www.albertwhitman.com.

With gratitude to Gertrude Chandler Warner,
who guides my steps through Greenfield,
and Deborah Warren, who walks by my side
on every new journey.

Contents

Chapter 1

Just Jessie?

Everything was on schedule. As I headed across the backyard, I even had a second to pause and admire the sign of my newfound freedom: a perfectly angled 8½" × 11" rectangle made of repurposed plywood.

> **JUST JESSIE**
>
> 10:00 A.M.
> TO 12:00 P.M.
>
> EVERY SATURDAY

At first I'd been worried about the idea. After all, ever since the day my brothers, sister, and I came to live with our grandfather, the old boxcar in our backyard had been our family hangout. For a short time, it had also been our home. That was before Grandfather found us and brought us to live with him. But things were different now. School had just started back up, and I was in seventh grade, which meant I was already halfway through middle school and even more than halfway to college. It was time to finally have some space for myself.

I'd come to our big family meeting ready to defend my decision. I'd made a presentation board that had a big *12* on top to remind everyone that I was practically a teenager. Pictures and graphs represented all the things that I was planning for the upcoming year—coursework, extracurriculars, sports, social life—and the estimated time I would need per week for each of them.

But the meeting ended up only lasting about three minutes, and two of those were spent cleaning up after my six-year-old brother, Benny, who spilled orange juice all over my desk. Basically, after I said what I wanted, everyone agreed right away, and they spent the rest of the afternoon helping me make my sign. Sometimes I forget that my family is pretty awesome about stuff like this.

The clock said 9:59.

In less than sixty seconds, I'd officially have the boxcar all to myself. I took one last look at the sign, the symbol of my independence, and slid open the door. The familiar squeak and clatter were music to my ears.

"If we're going to hang out back here, you've gotta get that thing oiled," my best friend, Charla Gray, said as she came into the yard through the back gate.

She was early. I had planned to have a little time in the boxcar before my Just Jessie time turned into Jessie and Charla Together time. But honestly, I wasn't even a little disappointed at the change in plans. The whole point was to focus on the important things in my life. And Charla was definitely important.

"Oil? No way," I replied with a laugh. "It's part of the atmosphere." I shoved the door all the way open, letting the final rattle hang in the silence between us.

"I suppose I'll get used to it," Charla said, nudging past me to be the first inside. "Even if I still think it's crazy that you have a literal *boxcar* in your backyard."

I followed her in, turned on the floor lamp, and closed

the door behind us. Charla tossed her backpack on the floor. She zipped off her sweatshirt, revealing a T-shirt that said "My Head's in the Cloud." It was a joke about online cloud storage and one of Charla's favorite shirts. She had a full wardrobe of computer-related clothing.

I was wearing a comfy, striped sweater that was a hand-me-down from my fourteen-year-old brother, Henry. I'd braided back my long brown hair and let my ten-year-old sister, Violet, tie a striped bow around the end. It made my outfit look a bit more intentional, rather than just easy, which was my normal style.

With a *whoosh*, Charla plopped into the beanbag in the corner. I headed to my desk and hit the power button on my computer. It began to boot up.

"Small pocket inside the big compartment," I told Charla before she had even asked a question.

"Huh?" Charla looped her backpack strap over her foot and dragged it across the floor to her. The zipper clicked softly as she opened the big compartment. "Ah, yep. There it is!" She pulled out her favorite pen—the one I'd given her with the purple pom-pom on top. "Now, where are my—" she began.

"Top of your head."

Charla had gotten her first-ever pair of glasses the week before. She was supposed to wear them all the time, but so far she mostly only put them on when she was using a computer. Which, come to think of it, was pretty much all the time anyway.

She reached up and found her new glasses twisted in her thick, dark curls. "Oh," she chuckled. "I wish I had your superpower."

"Oh, that," I replied with a sigh. Unfortunately, I knew exactly what she was talking about. My siblings and I had developed a bit of a reputation around our hometown of Greenfield, Connecticut. We were the kids who hung out in a boxcar and solved mysteries. It hadn't done wonders for my social life to say the least.

"It's not a superpower or even a little magic, Charla. I just notice small things others might not see," I explained. "You came to do homework with me. It was only natural that after you sat down, you'd need a pen. And your glasses." I added, "You left your notebook in my room last night. Here it is." I tossed the spiral-bound pad to her. "See? Just observant. That's all."

Charla opened the notebook, set her glasses on her nose, and raised her pen. "Well, you're super to me." She

5

laughed and tapped the pen on a piece of paper. "We have two whole hours! This is so exciting. What are you going to work on first? I was thinking I'd do math."

"Now there's a surprise," I said with a smirk. Math was Charla's favorite subject. "I have some research to do for my first history paper, so I think I'll start there."

But when I looked at my computer screen, all I saw was the spinning death wheel going around and around. I frowned. "That's not good."

"Move," Charla commanded. She pushed me away from the computer, pressed a couple of buttons all at once, waited a minute, pressed a couple more, then stepped away. "You're back." She added, "You really need a new laptop."

"I know," I said. "I'm saving my allowance, but until I can afford something else, I've got you." I opened the website. "Computers are *your* superpower."

Charla grinned. "Well, I'm glad you stink at computer stuff. I couldn't handle the competition." She thought about it and added, "I get you're trying to get away from the whole mystery-solving thing—which, by the way, I still think is awesome—but what do you think you might do instead? There are some clubs at school you could try out."

"*Too many* clubs." I held out my phone to show where I'd typed a list of everything our school offered. I'd hoped one of the groups would jump out at me, like coding did for Charla, but so far I couldn't see myself joining any of them. "I really want to be part of *something* though. I think I'll go to a few different meetings next week." It was a month into school, and a lot of the clubs had already started, but they still had informational sessions for kids who hadn't decided yet—kids like me.

"Awesomesauce." Charla settled back into the bean-bag. She was quiet for a second, then said, "I can't stop thinking about the storm."

Charla and I had talked about the storm that had hit a couple of days before about a million times already. Our garage had flooded, but a lot of people had bigger problems. I'd heard that some of the businesses on Main Street were damaged, but I hadn't gone out yet to see for myself.

In all the times Charla and I had talked, I hadn't mentioned that I had been scared during the storm. Now I admitted, "I got nervous when the electricity went out." Violet and I share a room where we have twin beds. After the power had shut off, Violet and our wire-haired terrier, Watch, had jumped into *my* bed and hid under the covers with me.

"What about Henry?" Charla asked.

"Oh," I chuckled. "He slept through it."

"How is that possible?!" Charla asked. "The thunder was *so* loud."

"He said he was tired." I laughed harder. Henry had always been a very sound sleeper.

"The thunder and lightning were scary, but the pounding rain made it even worse," Charla said. She also hadn't admitted she was scared until now. "My cat hid in the closet. He didn't even want to come out for treats." Pippen was like a cat version of my brother Benny. They were both always hungry.

"Wow, Pippen must have been so scared." Even Benny, as frightened as he was, had used a flashlight to get to the kitchen. He made his own "snack storm," which meant he ate raisins every time there was thunder and pretzel sticks each time lightning flashed across the sky. I knew all about it because he'd brought his snack bowl and climbed into my bed too.

It had been a long night, to say the least.

"Grandfather said a storm like that is super rare,"

I told Charla. She was new to Greenfield, while Grandfather had lived in town his whole life. "He was in high school the last time it stormed that hard. He said it was so bad the town had a big fundraiser to help fix up the damaged buildings and houses."

"I wonder if anyone is doing that this time," said Charla. "I'm sure there are people who could use help and—"

There was a knock on the boxcar door, then I heard Benny's voice. "Jessie! Hey, Jessie! Jessie, Jessie, Jess—"

I opened the door a crack and immediately saw the mop of shiny brown hair that belonged to my little brother. "Benny, you promised. It hasn't even been half an hour yet."

"But…" Benny looked back over his shoulder and lowered his voice. "There's a boy here. He said it's important." He went on. "I told him I couldn't let him see you unless it was a horrible, tragic, blood-gushing emergency. But he brought a bag of cookies, and you know…" Benny wiped crumbs off his shirt. "Ta-da! Here he is."

With a disappointed sigh, I opened the door a little wider to see the boy Benny had escorted to the boxcar.

"Daniel?"

Daniel Garza was in my art class. Since I always sat in the front while he always sat in the back, I'd never really talked to him. In fact, I wasn't sure I'd ever heard his voice.

Benny scooted back to the house, leaving Daniel in the yard. The sun was shining, but the grass still smelled like rain.

Charla leaned past me. "Don't just stand there," she said in a hushed voice. "Let him in!"

I put up a finger to Daniel, said "Hang on," and closed the rickety door behind us. "I bet he wants me to help him solve some kind of problem, like finding his missing cat," I said.

"What? Really?" Charla asked. "Why do you think that?"

I leaned against the boxcar door. "Trust me," I said. "This is *always* how it starts. Someone comes to the boxcar with a problem they need help with. Before long, everyone is talking about mysteries and pulling out their magnifying glasses and listing off clues and suspects." I took a deep breath before continuing. "And even if it *were* a real mystery, I'm not doing that anymore."

Charla was unfazed by my rant. "Well, I wish he were here to see me," she said in a dreamy voice. "I think he's cute, in a quiet, shy, adorable way. Did you see how his hair flops over one perfect dark-brown eye? I bet he doesn't need glasses to see!"

Wait, what? I had no idea my best friend had a crush on Daniel Garza!

"He's here to see *you*," Charla said eagerly. "*We* should let him in."

"I don't want to," I said firmly, then softened. "Do I have to?"

"He might have more cookies," Charla suggested. Then she gave me a playful shove to the side and opened the boxcar door.

Chapter 2

Definitely Not a Mystery

"Uh, hi." Daniel stepped into the boxcar but didn't raise his eyes from his shoes, which were white and dotted with mud from the yard.

"Come in." Charla pulled him inside and closed the boxcar door. It shut with a thud.

We all stood there looking at each other. No one spoke. It felt like forever before Charla said, "So, about that storm…"

"Yeah" was all Daniel said.

"Yeah," Charla echoed.

This was so awkward! I considered asking Daniel

if he'd been scared when the lights went out, or if his parents' shop in town had been damaged, or even just why he was there, when suddenly Daniel gasped.

"You like Hop-Man?" His voice was loud and clear, which was a little shocking.

"No, I—" I thought he was talking to me, but he wasn't. Awkward! He was talking to Charla.

Hop-Man was a half-frog, half-human superhero Charla loved. I thought the whole idea of a frog that stopped crimes with his sticky tongue was absurd, but she insisted it was no weirder than a teenager who could sling spiderwebs.

Charla's eyes followed Daniel's to her backpack. The latest issue of *Hop-Man* was sticking out the top of her bag. "Have you read this one?" Charla asked him, scooping up the comic book and holding it tenderly, as if it was her most precious possession.

"Read it?" Daniel's eyes raised from the floor for the first time since he'd entered the boxcar. "I memorized it!"

"Really?" Charla tested him, reciting a line: "'Is that a cape you're wearing?'"

"'No, it's a *jumpsuit*!'" Daniel replied.

They both began laughing, then they started hopping around the boxcar chanting, "Hop away! Hop away!"

There was a little part of me that wished I could be sillier and more impulsive like Charla, but it just wasn't in me. Noting that neither of them was watching where they were hopping, I grabbed my laptop and moved to a safe spot out of their way.

Once they were both out of breath, they took a break and Daniel asked Charla what she thought about the new villain in the latest issue.

I knew that if Charla got started talking about Hop-Man, we'd never get back to homework. "So, Daniel, what's up?" I cut in. It didn't take any special observation skills to figure out that he was here for a reason.

"Oh, right!" Daniel said, regaining focus. "I came to tell you something interesting that happened."

"Go on," I encouraged him. It looked like he hadn't come to tell me about a missing cat or to pitch a mystery to solve. He hadn't known that Charla was there, so he hadn't come to start a Hop-Man fan club either. He'd come to see me. That was terrific news! It was nice, friendly even, that he'd stopped by to share a story.

"A few months ago, my parents opened a store on Main Street," Daniel said.

As the new kid in school, Daniel was usually super shy, and even when he'd first entered the boxcar, he'd barely looked at us, but now he started talking a mile a minute.

"It's an art store," Daniel continued. I already knew about the shop. Violet was an artist and loved going there to look at the paintings. The store also offered classes and sold some art supplies. But before I could share all that, Daniel barreled on.

"I like to help out. I go there after school, plus weekends. It's fun to answer the phone and make deliveries." Here he lifted his hand to his ear, imitating what answering the phone looked like. "The morning after the storm, someone placed a pretty big order from us. Five paintings by one artist."

"That's great," Charla managed to cut in. "A big sale, and it came at a time when the store could probably really use the extra money."

"Yeah, the sale was good," Daniel agreed. "But they never came to even see what they were buying. All he said was"—Daniel raised his invisible phone to his ear again and said in a low, husky voice—"'Bring the paintings to this address.'"

"This all sounds pretty normal to me," I said, relieved there was no mystery hidden in his story. "Someone likes a particular artist and wanted their artwork."

"That's the thing, Jessie. It wasn't normal at all," Daniel countered. "It all came from one artist, but that's only because the buyer asked for the five most expensive pieces of art in the store," he said. "They didn't even ask if the paintings were landscapes or fruit bowls or modern splashes of color. They didn't ask anything at all."

"Maybe the buyer knew about the artist," I said, trying to provide a reasonable explanation. "They probably knew the kind of stuff they made."

"Just because you like the burgers a chef makes, it doesn't mean you'll also like her lasagna," Daniel explained. "And the buyer never mentioned the artist's name, just the high cost of the paintings."

"He makes a good point," Charla told me. "This art-sale thing sounds a little weird."

"It gets stranger," Daniel said, pacing across the

boxcar as he spoke. "I took the paintings, which were really big and heavy, to the address. There was a restaurant sign in front of the building, but the place had clearly been shut down for a while. The hinges on the front doors were rusty, and cobwebs filled the windows, but the door was unlocked."

I glanced at Charla, who was totally immersed in the tale. She was staring at Daniel, eyes wide. "Then what happened?" she asked.

"I went inside," he said. "On the dusty counter was an envelope with a check inside and a slip of paper with a phone number." He quickly added, "Hardly anyone uses checks anymore. Most purchases are made with credit cards or electronic payments. But that wasn't even the strangest part."

"I'm getting goose bumps," Charla said, rubbing her arms.

I'll admit I was impressed by Daniel's storytelling abilities, especially because this was the most I had ever heard him talk at once. Still, I wasn't sure where this story was headed.

"I called the number on the piece of paper," Daniel continued, once again taking out his make-believe phone and dialing. He went back to that husky voice. "'Leave the paintings. Take the check.'" He turned to me. "Weird, right?"

It looked like Daniel was waiting for me to answer, so I repeated the highlights. "Someone hired you to deliver paintings. You took them to the right location, left them where the buyer wanted them, and got paid." It might not have been the most modern form of payment, but a lot of people still used checks—people like Grandfather and all his friends.

"I knew you'd understand!" Daniel said, not getting that the story sounded like a totally normal sales interaction. "People say you're the best at getting to the bottom of these kinds of things."

"Oh." My shoulders sunk. Of course he hadn't come just to share a story. He wanted me to investigate something for him. I'd only just recently stopped solving mysteries and already I was rusty. It shouldn't have taken me so long to figure out why Daniel had come. I wanted things to be different so badly that I'd let my guard down.

"Oh no!" Charla said, grabbing Daniel's arm and pulling him into a corner.

"What?" Daniel asked. "Did I do something wrong?"

The two of them huddled in the shadows, whispering, but the boxcar was small and I could hear them clearly.

"Jessie isn't really doing that whole detective thing anymore," Charla told Daniel.

"But she's good at it," Daniel said softly to Charla. Then he figured out that I could hear them and turned to face me. "You are, you know. Good at solving stuff."

Charla said, "It's not a question of if she's good, because she's the best, she just—"

I needed to explain myself. "I'm trying to find my own thing, Daniel," I cut in. "No offense, but there's not even really a mystery here to solve." Again, I reviewed what I'd heard. "Your family got paid for an art delivery. That's not weird at all."

"But it *was* weird!" Daniel insisted. He added, "I thought this boxcar clubhouse was like…your mystery-solving office. Am I wrong?"

I sighed. "It was, but it's not anymore. At least not for me. I can go get my brother Henry if you want to tell him your story. But"—I clicked my tongue—"I'm going to bet that he'll tell you exactly the same thing I did.

There's no mystery to solve."

"Hang on." Charla held up a finger to Daniel and dragged me over near my computer. She pulled up a blank document so we could type to each other without Daniel hearing.

"We gotta help," Charla spelled out on the page.

"With what?" I typed back.

It was like texting, but we were standing next to each other using the same keyboard.

"Can't we go down to the restaurant and snoop around?" Charla suggested. "It would be like looking for bugs in a computer program, things that just don't look right."

I didn't know if Charla was really interested in helping Daniel or just wanted a way to spend more time with him.

"Charla," I typed quickly, "trust me. There's no mystery here. No bugs in the program."

"Okay." Charla was disheartened but seemed to get it.

We deleted the document and went back to Daniel. He'd been looking at Charla's Hop-Man comic book while waiting for us.

"What do you think?" Daniel asked me.

"Sorry." I shook my head. Last year or even just last month before school started, I might have said yes, but now I was on a different path. "I can't help."

My answer was final.

Daniel took in my reply. "It's okay," he said. "Bye." To make things even more awkward, he struggled to open the boxcar door to leave. The wood was swollen from the rain, and it stuck partway down the track.

Charla reached around him and slid open the door. She said, "Daniel, if anything else happens, anything strange at all, you should definitely let us know." She looked back at me, then added, "Seriously, let us know right away."

"Sure," Daniel muttered, having lost all the excitement in his voice. "Uh, see you both at school."

As he walked away, I could feel his disappointment. I was disappointed too. Change was hard, and I was working hard at changing. Even if there had been something strange about Daniel's story, I couldn't solve mysteries forever, right? It was time to move on.

I pushed past Charla to close the boxcar door. It rolled back into place and clunked shut.

I glanced at the clock. Only fifty-three minutes

remained of our special time. It was just enough to start my history research before Henry, Violet, and Benny showed up.

"Now it's officially Jessie and Charla Together time." I smiled. "Let's do homework."

Chapter 3

A New Lead

"Did you hear the news?" Charla was standing in front of my locker when I arrived at school on Monday. She was wearing a T-shirt with a floppy disk printed on it. I had on the same sweater I'd worn on Saturday.

The hallway was mostly empty. We both liked to get to school early. That's how we met, actually. On the first day, we'd been the only ones in the hall. Charla had borrowed my roll of tape to put up some decorations in her locker. I could tell she liked to be prepared as much as I did, which meant our friendship was pretty much meant to be.

"Your grandfather was right!" Charla went on, answering her own question. She handed me a flyer. "There's going to be a citywide fundraiser in a couple of weeks for the people affected by the storm."

"Just like when Grandfather was a kid," I said. On the way to school, he'd driven down Main Street. The damage was even worse than I'd expected. There were lots of windows that now had plywood in the frames. Grandfather had noticed one of his friends sweeping glass off the sidewalk in front of the hardware store. He'd said he was going to go back and help out after he dropped me off.

"I think it's a great idea," Charla said, pointing to the flyer. "There's going to be an auction and a charity concert. But little events are going to help too. Everyone around town is going to pitch in. After all the money is collected, the businesses that need the money most will get help."

I thought about Grandfather's friend. I didn't know if he could afford new windows or not. I hoped he would get money from the fundraiser if he needed it.

I read the flyer carefully. It said our school, Greenfield Middle, was going to sell candy bars to help out. The person who sold the most candy would get a certificate at the citywide event.

"I bet Benny will use all his allowance to buy some chocolate bars," I said. "I could probably win that certificate just by selling to him. It's for a good cause, of course."

We both laughed.

Lucinda Dawson came down the hallway with her best friend, Victoria Kim, following close behind. Lucinda's locker was next to mine. I didn't know her very well, but I knew that Charla didn't like her at all. The first week of school, Charla had wanted to join Girls with Goals, a club Lucinda had started. The club was going to do helpful projects around town. Charla had texted Lucinda for information. They'd been pretty friendly in sixth grade, so it was a surprise when Lucinda never replied. Now Charla thought Lucinda didn't want her in Girls with Goals.

Three weeks later, even though Charla had joined coding club and never talked about Girls with Goals again, I knew it still upset her.

"Hey, Jessie!" Lucinda called my name before I'd finished sorting my books. "I see you've seen the news about the fundraiser. My dad is helping to arrange the whole thing, but Girls with Goals is also putting together a special event to help clean up the mess from the flood at Pickhardt Park."

Charla was right next to me, but Lucinda didn't look at her. This was the first time I'd seen them together, and Lucinda really did seem to be ignoring Charla.

"Hope you'll come." Lucinda grabbed a fuzzy purple sweater from her locker and shut the door. She always looked like she was about to enter a movie set, with perfect hair that curled around her face and shiny lip gloss. Victoria had the same sweater in powder blue, the same curls, and the same glistening lips. Glancing toward Charla, Lucinda said coolly, "You can come too if you want."

As they walked away, Lucinda told Victoria, "We'll need gloves and trash cans. Let's use social media to spread the word."

"I know you're not into Lucinda," I said to Charla while we headed to class in the other direction. "But she definitely knows her *thing*."

"Yeah. She knows how to ghost someone." Charla sighed. "I don't understand her at all."

"I only meant she's a good organizer," I explained.

Charla said, "Now that is a mystery someone should look into. Who knows what's behind that perfect look and her do-gooder club?"

"I see…so now *you* want me to be a detective too?" I lowered my eyes at Charla and nodded toward Daniel, who was already inside the art room. He hadn't looked up at us as we walked in, concentrating on his assignment instead. He'd clearly been there awhile and had gotten a jump on the project.

"Forget it. I just want you to be you," Charla told me. I knew she'd never ask me to solve a mystery for her, but I'd definitely do it if she needed me to. She was my best friend, and that's what best friends do. She sighed. "I just wish I knew why Lucinda doesn't like me."

"You could ask her," I said for the billionth time. "You don't need a detective if you can ask."

"Oh, I tried that," Charla said. "Remember? I texted. I called her once too. I even waited for her after school. She'd talk to me about other stuff, but not the club. Finally, I gave up asking."

When Charla stopped mentioning that she wanted to be in Girls with Goals, I'd forgotten all she'd gone through. We hardly ever saw Lucinda anyway. We were always early to school, and Lucinda was always late. We were rarely at our lockers at the same time and didn't have any classes together.

I couldn't help but wonder just what the reason was for Lucinda being so weird to Charla. The way she'd only sort of invited Charla to the park cleanup felt like she hadn't really wanted to invite her at all.

Why was Lucinda—? Wait! No! I pushed Lucinda's strange behavior out of my head. I was not going to obsess about it.

New school year. New day. New Jessie.

"You don't need to investigate anything," Charla told me. "I already know why she ignores me," she said at last. "I'm like Hop-Man's chameleon sidekick." She waved her hands in front of my face. "I blend into my surroundings. You can't see me, can you?"

"*Charla*-meleon?" I chuckled. "Hate to break it to you, but I can see you just fine."

"Darn." Charla frowned. "Okay, well, that's not it then." She pulled out her art supplies. "I'd rather have a different superpower anyway," she said. "I think I'd like to fly."

"I'd just like to be able to paint," I said, gathering my own empty palette, some brushes, and a sheet of paper. "I'm going to get an F in this class. Well, probably more like a B minus, but still."

We'd already learned basic brushstroke techniques and how to mix colors. Today we were moving on to creating watercolor landscapes.

Every student had to take one art class at school. It could be drawing, painting, or pottery. It was simply coincidence that Charla and I had both picked painting. For Daniel, painting seemed like the obvious choice, since his parents owned the art store and everything.

Charla thought learning about art and color would help her if she ever wanted to try computer animation. But for me, it was just a required class I had to take in my first semester. In three months, it would be over and we'd move on to a music elective instead. I'd already decided to take the class called Music Appreciation. No instrument required.

Thankfully, for this art project, our teacher, Mr. Masoud, didn't want us to get all caught up in creative details. He just wanted us to focus on technique. That's why we were going to do our best to copy a famous artist's work.

The painting was projected on the wall.

I quickly memorized the details and mentally divided the artwork into manageable parts. Because watercolor paintings are layered, there were many possible starting points. I decided to begin at the bottom and systematically paint my way toward the top.

I dipped my brush in the water. I needed to mix the color of the land in the landscape. It was meant to look like soil, but my brown mixture became too dark and came out like tar. I added a bit of white. Then it was too light, so I added purple. That made the color look like rotten grapes. I wished Violet would walk in and help. She was the artist of the family.

Frustrated, I wiped my forehead with the back of my hand. Charla laughed, and being a good friend, she told me to wash my face instead of letting me walk around all day at school with a smudge that looked like rotten grapes.

I went to get a wet paper towel, and when I returned, I said, "Art definitely isn't going to be my new thing."

"Want to come to coding club after school?" Charla asked. "We're starting a new project today. I could catch you up." She swished her brown paint mixture onto her paper and then began blending a pretty shade of orange. "I was thinking I could help our school raise money by inventing a life-size robot that could sell candy bars door-to-door."

"Really?" My orange color was too red.

"Nah. I'm joking." Charla laughed. "I'm not that good *yet*. But I think I might be able to design a simple app to track sales."

"Less impressive than a robot," I replied. "A good idea though." I'd tried coding once in an online class. None of the programs I wrote had worked quite right. I was in awe of Charla. Everything she programmed worked perfectly.

When class was nearly over, Mr. Masoud came around to look at the projects.

"Lovely," I heard him say to Libby, a girl in the back.

"You're very talented," he told Daniel. "Must run in the family."

"Nice job," he said to Charla. I glanced over. Her

painting looked a lot like the famous one we were copying. I was impressed.

Mr. Masoud stopped at my desk. He stared at my work for a few beats, then said, "A fine effort, Jessie."

I studied my artwork, trying to see what he saw. My eyes went from my painting to the famous artwork that was still on the projector. The original was beautiful. Fertile brown land stretched across the bottom. Green trees reached up toward the sky. A sunset crossed the horizon. There was a small lake, a few birds, and a hot air balloon in the distance.

When I first heard about the assignment, I'd thought that imitating a famous artist would be easy, but it had turned out to be super hard. My land looked like sludge. My sunset was a melted popsicle. The lake was mossy, and my birds looked like they were falling out of the sky. I had added a hot air balloon, but it was deflated and would have been a terrifying ride.

"Fine effort!" I echoed my teacher's compliment. Grades were based on effort, not skill, so hurrah for me. "Thank you," I told Mr. Masoud.

"Do you have your group arranged for the next project?" he asked. Mr. Masoud was bald and had glasses. He always wore a beret, as if he'd dropped out of a French art school and headed directly to our classroom.

"I'm with Charla," I said.

"I thought you might say that," he told me. "But we have an extra student in the room. I'd like you and Charla to take on a third partner." I followed his eyes to the back of the room where Daniel sat.

Daniel raised his gaze from the floor just long enough to wave at me and Charla.

Charla waved back. I didn't, but it wasn't because I was against having Daniel join our group. As long as he didn't tell me any more mystery painting stories, or any mystery stories at all, I was happy to work with him.

The reason I didn't wave was because I'd noticed something as Mr. Masoud collected our paintings. When he lifted mine off the desk, the newspaper I'd spread out to protect the surface had caught my eye.

The latest edition of the *Greenfield Gabber*, our school paper, stared up at me. Its printed columns were smeared with my colorful brushstrokes, but I could still read the most important part.

MEETING FOR NEW JOURNALISTS

- Do you have an eye for detail?
- Do you love to write?
- Are you curious about the world around you?
- Do you want to make a difference?

Join the *Greenfield Gabber*!

The student newspaper is looking for new journalists and will have an informational session at 3:00 p.m. this coming Monday.

That was today!

I quickly tore off the notice and showed it to Charla. "What do you think?" I asked her.

She looked at the paper, then turned to me with a huge smile. Charla tapped her finger on the word *journalist* and declared, "Now *this* could be your thing!"

Chapter 4

The Gabber

"Daniel's a good artist, right?" Charla asked.

It was the end of the school day. Charla and I were having a quick snack together before club time. I'd brought some of the cookies Daniel had left at my house the day before, which were surprisingly delicious.

"Very good artist," I mumbled between bites.

"Working with him means we'll get a high grade for sure," Charla gushed.

"Very high," I repeated.

"I like potatoes," Charla said.

"Yes, potatoes," I mumbled.

"Jessie Alden!" Charla exclaimed. "You aren't listening to me at all!"

"Sorry." I turned to face Charla. I honestly thought I'd been faking it pretty well, but Charla saw through my act. "I'm listening with half my brain," I told her. "The other half is thinking about the school newspaper."

"I'm glad you're excited," Charla said. She crossed her fingers. "I really hope it ends up being a good fit for you."

"Me too," I said, offering her the last cookie as an apology. "I promise I'll be a better listener."

"Next time, I'll just talk louder!" Charla shouted jokingly. She took the cookie. "I'll make sure you hear EVERY WORD clearly."

As I laughed, I noticed Daniel walking toward us. "Uh...why are you yelling?" he asked as he approached. He had the hood of his sweatshirt pulled up over his head so we couldn't see his face very well.

Charla blushed, then stuffed the whole cookie awkwardly in her mouth so she couldn't speak.

"We were testing my hearing," I said as I pointed toward my ear. "It's good."

"Uh, okay," Daniel said. This was school Daniel, not the animated guy we'd met yesterday. He looked like he would run away if he had to stand with us for even another second.

Charla was still chewing, so I said, "The group project is a mural. Do you have any ideas for what we should do?" We could use mixed media as long as we stuck with the theme: animals and their habitats.

"I like zebras," Charla said after swallowing hard.

"Same," Daniel said.

I rolled my eyes at the two of them. We needed the fast-talking Daniel from the boxcar to come back, and then we had to get rid of crushing-on-Daniel Charla. This group project would be a lot easier if everyone acted normal and we were all just friends.

"Looks like we're doing zebras," I said. "Maybe we could illustrate a savannah? We could work in something about protecting the environment?"

"I like it," Charla said. "What do you think, Daniel?"

"Cool." He nodded. "We can use the studio at the shop. All the supplies we need are already there." He pushed back his hoodie and glanced from Charla to me. "Is tonight okay? My mom can order us a pizza."

I looked though my planning calendar. I had a little homework but not too much. "I'm free," I said. "I'll pick up some books on zebras from the school library on the way out."

"All right." Daniel threw his hoodie back up and walked away.

I left Charla at the computer lab and headed into the newspaper room.

Ms. Surovsky, my English teacher, was also the teacher in charge of the club. I hadn't known she was the liaison, but seeing her made the club even more exciting. She'd been my favorite teacher so far this year.

She had midnight-dark hair that fell in tight ringlets and wore glasses that hung on a beaded chain around her neck. Sometimes I wondered if she even needed the glasses at all. I'd never seen her wear them.

I felt a rush of excitement as Ms. Surovsky explained the different sections of the newspaper. The room was packed with people. There were older students who had been on the paper staff before. They'd been the ones who got the first edition out. Then there were a few students like me—newbies—who were here to see if we wanted to join the club.

The more Ms. Surovsky explained how things worked, the more interested I became. "We will have several journalists writing stories each week," she said. "We rotate who writes for each edition. Getting a paper out every other Monday is hard. If you want to be part of the staff, you'll need dedication."

I saw one of the girls in the back gather her things. Clearly, she didn't want to work so hard. But I did!

There would be articles assigned about sports teams, classes, or changes at the school. There'd also be assignments to write short biographies about one teacher and one student each month. After those pieces, there was room for us to pitch pretty much anything we wanted to work on. The pitched pieces would be called features.

I loved the idea of being a feature writer. I had a lot of experience asking strangers questions, and note-taking came naturally. If Ms. Surovsky agreed, we could choose our own topics, and we didn't have space limits either. The articles could be as long as they needed to be to fairly cover the story.

The sports, class, and biography assignments went to seasoned reporters for the next issue. Ms. Surovsky was going to do the first feature herself, since those took the longest to prepare. New reporters had two weeks to get a feel for the club before they had to start writing.

When Ms. Surovsky asked for other ideas, a boy I knew from history class asked if he could do something about the food in the cafeteria, which, he said, was way better than at his last school.

"Sounds good," said Ms. Surovsky. "But it will probably be quite a while until it gets published, okay?"

The boy nodded.

"I want you to interview the cafeteria workers," Ms. Surovsky told him. "Get to know them. Find out why they chose to work in our school and what they dream about." She added, "Then, once you truly understand how the cafeteria works, you can review the menu."

He agreed and started writing ideas for interview questions in his notebook.

I felt a rush of joy. His article wasn't going to be a fluff piece about chicken nuggets. Ms. Surovsky was pushing him, and all of us, to get deep into our stories and find new angles to report.

I raised my hand.

"Yes, Jessie?"

"I know it's my first day, but I'd really like to write something that could make a difference," I said.

"Like what?" She encouraged me to explain.

"The Girls with Goals club is doing a cleanup day in a park that was damaged in Friday's storm." I knew this would be an interesting topic that might make more people want to help around town.

"I'm not convinced yet," she said, raising an eyebrow. "There will already be articles about the school's fund-raising sale. What makes your story special?"

She was challenging me. I thought hard about it before I answered. "Girls with Goals is a student-led club. The candy bar fundraiser is run by adults. I'd like to explore how kids my own age, kids from our school, can help repair the storm damage in Greenfield."

"It's a very good idea, Jessie." Ms. Surovsky smiled. "There are so many clubs on campus, but I've never heard of that one. I'd be interested in reading what you discover." She nodded at me and said, "You have two weeks from today to get the article to me." Ms. Surovsky stood up and looked at all of us eager journalists and announced, "Welcome to the *Greenfield Gabber*."

Chapter 5

Damage Done

From the moment Daniel met us at the door of his parents' shop, I knew he was back to being Not-School Daniel. He was super chatty, and when Charla noted the broken window that had been boarded with plywood, he launched into a detailed account of the cleanup.

"We actually came in the middle of the night," he said. "When the window broke, the shop's security alarm went off."

"Really?" Charla asked, taking a slice of cheese pizza Daniel had ordered.

"The alarm company called us at home. Dad knew it wasn't a burglar, but wind and water in a store that sells mostly paper stuff is a disaster, so my mom and dad woke me up. We all got in the car and drove here as fast as we could.

"It was scary. Water was everywhere and more was rushing in fast." Daniel pointed to the walls and the floors. "Mom and I started moving the art to the back room, while Dad fought the storm and sealed the window with plastic and tape."

It was quite a story, made extra dramatic by Daniel's telling of it. I had to admit, Not-School Daniel had a knack for making things interesting.

He went on. "We used towels we'd brought from home to dry everything we could and stacked the art and supplies out of the way. While we were at school today, people came around town and helped to board up the shops. There was so much damage that the hardware store ran out of wood."

I wondered which stores Grandfather had volunteered to help. He was really handy with a hammer, and helping people was definitely his thing.

"People can be really nice!" Charla said, grabbing a

soda from a cooler. She handed me one too. I picked up a slice of pizza for myself and looked around, taking in details. It looked like after they fixed the window, the carpet would need to be replaced, and some of the walls might need to be repainted—or even replaced if the drywall had gotten wet. Water damage is really messy. And I had heard Grandfather say, the repairs could be expensive too.

Daniel got some pizza for himself and continued talking as he ate. "Dad hopes the money raised by the town's fundraising might help us." He added, "Mom's worried it won't help enough. I guess the business was just starting to find its footing when all this happened."

"Oh, I hope you don't have to move," Charla said.

"Me too," Daniel replied. "I have a really hard time making friends." He sighed. "I get shy when I'm uncomfortable."

"That's hard to believe," Charla joked.

"Well," I said, "I'm glad you're comfortable with us." I really was glad. I liked Not-School Daniel. Maybe he'd eventually show this side of himself to the others at school. And since he hadn't mentioned the art mystery, I was feeling more like myself too. My new self.

We moved from the front room to the studio space at the back of the shop. A lot of the artwork Mr. and Mrs. Garza had moved was stacked against the walls, and supplies packed the shelves to overflowing. It was crowded, but I knew that was temporary.

Daniel had his own workspace in the corner, and we pulled three chairs around the long table. Charla moved aside a book called *Drawing Zoo Animals* and discovered a tall stack of Hop-Man drawings hidden underneath. "Are these your pictures?" she asked Daniel.

"Yeah." Daniel blushed. "I'm thinking about trying to be a comic book artist one day. I like to use Hop-Man to practice."

"This is amazing!" Charla gushed. "You could draw the day Hop-Man met the—"

I could see that Charla was about to get completely sidetracked.

"We need to figure out how to divide the work for the project," I put in. "Since Daniel is the best artist, I think he should pencil in the sketch." I set out the books I'd found in the school library. "I can make a list of the kinds of plants and animals that would be found in the environments our zebras live in. Maybe some interesting facts could be woven into the art?" I turned to Charla, who was staring at me like I'd crushed her comic book dreams. "What do you want to focus on?"

"Hop-Man," she said sadly. "But I get it." She pushed out her bottom lip. "School comes first."

"We'll paint together," Daniel said. "It'll be fun."

We agreed on the plan and were about to get started brainstorming ideas when Daniel's mom popped her head into the room.

"Hi there," she greeted me and Charla. "I'm so glad that Daniel is making friends at school." Then she turned toward Daniel. "Sorry to interrupt, but do you have the phone number for that recent art delivery, the really big one?"

"No," Daniel said. "I tossed out the slip."

"The number is in your phone," I reminded him. "Whenever you make a call, the number is saved." At least that's how most phones worked.

"Jessie! You're a genius," Daniel gushed. He grabbed his cell, and sure enough, the number was right there. The call had only lasted a few seconds. "Are you sure you don't want to try solving this—"

"Positive," I said.

"Okay." He let it go, and I was grateful. Daniel gave the number to his mom, and she left the room, snatching a piece of pizza from the box on her way out.

"Now, what is it you both like about zebras?" I asked Daniel and Charla. But before they replied, Daniel's mom popped back into the room.

"You don't have another number, do you?" she asked her son.

Daniel raised an eyebrow. "No, why?"

She clicked her tongue. "This one's been disconnected."

"Let me try it," Daniel said, making the call directly from his own phone.

I could hear the *beep*, *beep*, *beep* and the announcement that the number was out of service.

Daniel hung up.

"I don't know what to do," his mom said with a long sigh. "Today, I went to cash the check for that delivery, and it didn't go through. We aren't getting paid for those five expensive paintings."

I tried very hard not to say anything that might sound like it was detective work, but she looked so sad, and Daniel looked so confused.

I couldn't help myself. I asked, "Do you have the

check, Mrs. Garza?" She pulled it from her pocket. "What's the name on it?"

"Johanna Blart," she told us. "I did a basic web search and can't find anyone by that name."

"Do you mind letting Charla try? If the woman who wrote the check exists, she'll find her," I said with certainty.

I was good at book research, but Charla was an internet pro. Mrs. Garza let Charla use the art shop's computer. Charla scrolled around a few websites, typing furiously and frowning the whole time. Finally, she announced the results. "I've pretty much hit the end of the internet. I don't think Johanna Blart ever really existed."

"Are you sure?" Daniel asked Charla.

"Positive," Charla said. She pointed at the screen. "Not in Greenfield or anywhere near here. I even looked to see if I could find a website for the old restaurant where Daniel delivered the paintings," she added, "but there isn't one. It's hard to not be *anywhere* online, but Johanna Blart just isn't showing up."

"That's what I thought," Mrs. Garza said. "I'd better go talk to your dad, Daniel." She thanked us, then left the shop.

After that, it was hard to focus on zebras.

"I think we need to investigate," Charla told me. Daniel didn't say anything out loud, but the expression on his face was perfectly clear: *I told you so!*

I thought about the situation. It was true. Things weren't looking good. The paintings had been delivered to an empty store where a check had been left on the table. But then the check turned out to be bad, and no one knew who'd left it. In fact, the person who had left the check didn't seem to exist at all.

If I *were* trying to solve a mystery, which I definitely wasn't, I'd go to the restaurant and see if the paintings were still there. If they were, then Daniel's family could take back the art and that would be the end. If the art was gone, though…well, I didn't want to consider that just yet.

I told Daniel and Charla all that, then added, "I'm sure there's a good explanation for what's going on. We just haven't figured it out yet."

"Then there's only one thing to do…" Charla began.

I had a bad feeling she wasn't going to say *spend the next hour working on our art project.*

"We have to go to the restaurant and see if the artwork is still there," Daniel said, finishing her thought.

I sighed. I could see that if we didn't go to the restaurant, we'd never get back to our homework, so I reluctantly agreed. Afterward, we could stop thinking about mysteries and get back to drawing zebras.

"We'll go tomorrow after school," I said. "But this does *not* mean I'm investigating. I'm just going with my friends to see a new, interesting spot in town."

"Like tourists," Charla said.

Daniel pretended he was our tour guide. "And to your left is an old, creepy abandoned building. The spiders are having a wonderful fly feast."

"Hop-Man would love that dinner menu," Charla said.

Charla and Daniel looked at each other and grinned.

With a loud groan, I picked up a book about zebras and pretended to read.

Chapter 6

The Restaurant

The school bell rang, marking the end of the school day. I knew Charla and Daniel were waiting for me by the front door, but I needed to stop at my locker first.

"Hey, Jessie." Lucinda was sorting through her binders. I'd somehow gone from never seeing her around to running into her pretty regularly. "Did you hear the news?"

I wasn't sure what she was talking about, so I shook my head.

"The candy bar sales!" Lucinda told me. "I've got the top spot on the school's leaderboard."

"That's terrific," I told her. It was the first official day of the sales, and I hadn't even started. I was amazed that Lucinda had been able to sell candy while we were in school all day.

"I know," Lucinda gushed. "Social media is my jam."

I noticed that Lucinda was wearing new red-and-yellow sandals that matched her belt and purse. "Cute outfit," I commented. Though I'd never wear something coordinated like that, it did look good on Lucinda.

I decided that this was the perfect time to ask her about my newspaper article. I was already pretty sure I knew how she would react, given how much she seemed to like attention, but I still wanted to see how she felt about the idea before I really started digging into it. "I want to write about Girls with Goals for the school paper," I told her.

"For the *Gobbler*?" Lucinda stood up a little straighter and threw back her hair. I wanted to tell her that I wasn't planning on taking photos to go with the article, but now wondered if maybe I should ask Ms. Surovsky if there was space for a picture or two. I had no doubt Lucinda would like to see herself in the paper.

"It's the *Gabber*," I corrected. "Can I talk to you about the club?"

"Meet me at the park cleanup this weekend," Lucinda said. "I can tell you all about it there. How I got the idea to make a club with my friends. How I got permission to start it. How I came up with the brilliant idea for the park cleanup."

"Sure," I said. "I'd like to hear all those stories. Plus," I added, "I have a few questions of my own."

"Of course," Lucinda said. "If there's time, I can answer them! It is a park cleanup, you know, so there will be a lot to get done."

"Right," I said. I'd follow Lucinda around with a trash bag all day if I had to, just to make sure I got the answers to all my questions.

"See you then," Lucinda told me. "And keep a close eye on the leaderboard! I plan to sell more candy bars than anyone in the city."

She took off for the parking lot, and I went out to meet Charla and Daniel.

"What took you so long?" Charla asked me as we began to walk toward the abandoned restaurant.

"Lucinda," I said.

"Ugh," she replied.

"I'm going to interview her for the paper," I admitted.

I figured it was best just to get that detail out in the open.

"Lucinda?!" Charla stopped walking and turned to face me. It was chilly out and her sweatshirt said "404 Not Found." That was the error message for when a website didn't load properly, or so Charla told me.

I zipped up my jacket and said, "I had an idea to write about Girls with Goals for the school newspaper. Ms. Surovsky thought it would make a good feature."

Charla sighed. I could tell she wanted to be supportive but also that it was hard when it came to Lucinda. "Yeah. It is a good topic. I just wish she weren't the person behind the club."

Maybe Charla was right about one thing. I might dig a little to see what had happened when Charla asked to join. Just a little. I realized that Lucinda had invited me to the park cleanup but not to join the club. That seemed interesting, but there was probably a reason for it as well.

I asked, "Charla, do you know how many people are even in that club?"

Charla shrugged. "Lucinda and Victoria…that's two."

"There have to be others," I said.

She shrugged again. "I *guess* you'll find out at the cleanup this weekend, eh?"

"And I *guess* you're not coming with me?" I knew the answer but thought I'd ask to see her reaction.

Charla pointed at her sweatshirt. "That, my friend, is a true four-oh-four error. Your question is so flawed that it's not even loading." She put her hands out like a robot and said, "Does not compute," in a mechanical voice.

Daniel had been walking ahead of us. He realized we'd stopped and waited for us to catch up. "What's going on?" he asked.

"Nothing," I said. "I'm writing an article for the school paper, and Charla is pretending she's a robot." That summed it up.

"Okay." Daniel accepted my explanation without any further questions. The wind blew and he tucked his hands into his jacket pockets. "We need to turn left here," he said.

The days were shorter in the fall. By the time we arrived at the abandoned restaurant, the sun was low in the sky. Daniel put up a hand, and we all stopped about a block away from our destination.

He took off his backpack. I had assumed he was carrying his homework, just like I was, but there wasn't a notebook or pen in sight. Instead, his pack was filled with supplies for our trip.

"Where are your books?" I asked, trying to ignore that this "tourist visit" to an abandoned restaurant was now looking like a top-secret mission.

"We don't need books. We need spy supplies." He handed me a flashlight, black gloves, and an oversize black shirt. "I didn't know your size," Daniel said. He gave Charla the same items, plus she got what appeared to be a minicamera hidden in a lipstick case. "I thought you'd like to be in charge of the tech for our mission."

"YES!" Charla cheered, checking out the camera. "I assume it has a USB port so we can upload the footage later?"

This was ridiculous. "Charla, you don't even wear lipstick, so faking it is just…fake!" I snorted. "And it's an abandoned building. What are you going to take photos of?" I knew I was ruining the fun for them, but seriously, is this what they thought detective work was like? They'd both clearly seen too many movies.

"We need to be prepared," Daniel said. "We don't know what kind of dangerous situation we're heading into."

"Ugh." I blew out a heavy breath as the two of them dressed for the investigation. I put the black

T-shirt into my backpack. I was NOT going along with this nonsense.

Charla and Daniel ignored my bad attitude and didn't comment on the fact that I put the gloves in my pocket. But when Daniel pulled black knit hats out of his backpack, he didn't bother to give me one. "Let's go," he whispered.

"No one is around," I said. "And it's barely dark enough to hide in the shadows like ninjas." The sky was tinged with the few final golden rays of the day.

They continued to ignore me, dodging toward the shadow of a dumpster, then behind a tree, and finally creeping up to the restaurant door.

I walked behind them like a normal person. It was hard not to laugh as Daniel peeked in the window of the building, then flopped to the ground, making himself flat like a pancake.

"Get down!" he hissed in a panicked tone. Charla pancaked herself next to him.

"Oh, come on…" I started, but Daniel grabbed my hand and pulled me down.

"There's someone in there," he whispered. He pointed to one of the two large windows that were next to the main door.

"I doubt—" I stopped talking as the beam of a flashlight suddenly came shining from inside the building. I didn't lay down on the sidewalk, but I squatted out of sight. I noticed there was a padlock on the door. In Daniel's original story, the door had been unlocked. I asked him to confirm.

"There wasn't a lock," he said, shaking his head. "That's new."

I wondered how someone could have gotten into the building with the front door now padlocked tight from the outside. There had to be a back door.

I gave in to the need for discretion. I put on the black T-shirt and asked Daniel for the hat.

He was practically glowing with delight when he handed it to me. "Gloves," he said, pointing to my bare hands. I rolled my eyes at him but pulled them out of my pocket and put them on anyway.

We used the cover of the darkening street to move around to the back of the building. I quietly repeated to myself over and over like a mantra, "Not a mystery. Not a mystery. Logical explanation. Logical explanation."

The back door to the restaurant was propped open with a brick. There was a dirty white van in the lot. We ducked behind the van, using it for cover and peeking around it to see what we could see.

"Let's go in," Charla said, adjusting her lipstick camera, ready for action.

"No way," I said, telling myself one more time that there was a logical explanation for someone being inside. Whoever owned the building might be in there. They probably didn't pay for electricity anymore. They—

Suddenly, Charla's phone rang. "Oh, my bad!" She flicked it off quickly, but whoever was inside had definitely heard the ringtone. The flashlight went off, plunging the building into darkness.

We sprinted to hide behind some nearby trees. From my hiding spot, I saw someone come outside, get into the white van we'd been standing behind only moments before, and speed away. I couldn't make out what the person looked like, but they were definitely in a hurry.

Once we were sure we were alone, Daniel rushed to the building's back door. "It's locked," he announced.

I launched into my reasons why nothing unusual had happened here tonight and how we had probably just frightened the person in the building. "Logical expl—" I was saying when Daniel unzipped his backpack.

He had one more trick in there. "This camera attachment for my phone will let us see inside," Daniel said.

"Experimental technology?" Charla asked. "Heat vision?"

"Just a really good flash bulb," Daniel said.

We returned to the front of the building. Daniel stuck his phone up against a window and took a series of photos, then we gathered around to look at them.

"Are those boxes?" Charla asked. The photo was super grainy and out of focus.

"I couldn't afford the phone with the better camera," he explained apologetically. "Or the military-grade spy gear I wanted."

He zoomed in on the photo, and we all took a second look. There were a lot of boxes, maybe ten or more in the picture. They were in piles, so it was hard to see how deep the stacks went.

"Looks like the paintings I delivered are gone," Daniel said.

I nodded. On closer examination, I recognized store names and logos printed on the sides of the boxes. "These seem to be from stores around town," I said.

"So we have someone sneaking around an abandoned

building at night in creepy white van, the name of someone who doesn't actually exist, a whole bunch of missing paintings, *and* a bunch of other random goods that are probably stolen," Charla pointed out. She stared hard at me. "Jessie, will you finally admit *this* is a mystery?"

"I'm sure there's a good explanation," I said. But as I spoke, I realized just how unconvincing I sounded. Truthfully, I was feeling less sure by the second.

Chapter 7

Questions and Answers

Saturday morning, I skipped Just Jessie time in the boxcar and instead went to Lucinda's Girls with Goals cleanup at Pickhardt Park. Henry, Violet, and Benny were excited to help out after the storm, so they came along too. I was excited to get out my phone and start taking notes for my first assignment.

The park had been closed to the public since the storm. It was a mess. Trash cans had tipped over. Garbage was littered across the grass and stuck in the plants. Some trees had broken branches that needed to be cut down. Leaves needed to be raked too. It was a big project, but there were a lot of people there to help.

We'd come prepared. Benny brought a box of trash bags. Henry had work gloves. Violet was dragging a cooler full of snacks and drinks that Grandfather had purchased for the volunteers.

"I wish we could have brought Watch," Benny said as we crossed the grass to where a small group was standing around. "He loves the park."

"It would have been too hard to keep an eye on him while we are cleaning up," Violet explained. "He also loves squirrels."

"And bunnies and birds and grasshoppers and butterflies," Benny added.

I laughed. Watch was well trained, but he could get distracted. Then again, so could my siblings.

"Hey, I see some friends from school," Henry told us. "They must have seen the event posted on the internet. I'm going to go say hi."

Benny and Violet also saw people they knew, and within a short time, I was heading to talk to Lucinda all by myself. One of the first things I noticed was that only Victoria and Lucinda were wearing Girls with Goals T-shirts—the glittery rhinestones outlining the *G*,

W, and *G* in *Girls with Goals* made it easy to spot them. Everyone else was in their regular clothes.

"It's a good turnout," I told Lucinda. She was standing with an older man, who was holding a park map that had been drawn over with colorful squares.

"There are more than fifty kids here!" she gushed. "And I heard even more might be on the way." She seemed very proud. "There are representatives from every school in town."

The man put his arm around Lucinda's shoulders. "That's my girl! Taking after her old man."

"Is this your dad?" I asked, even though it was obvious.

She introduced us. "Jessie is writing a feature on Girls with Goals for the school paper," Lucinda explained.

"I'd love to read it when you're done," Mr. Dawson told me. "I started as a newspaper journalist myself."

I immediately liked Lucinda's father. He told me he'd been a reporter at college while studying to be a civil engineer, which is someone who designs and plans big projects for cities, like roads and water systems. Now, he owned a company that designed and painted the markings on roads. I'd never met anyone who did that before.

"Every time you see a bike lane in Greenfield, you can thank my dad," Lucinda said.

"That's really interesting," I said, making a note of his job.

"I'm glad you think so," Mr. Dawson replied. "Most of Lucinda's friends get bored quickly when I talk about my job." He chuckled. "Excuse me, girls, but I see someone I need to say hi to."

Mr. Dawson walked away toward a worried-looking, gray-haired man who was pacing back and forth. "Hey there, Frank!" he shouted as he waved his hand in greeting. Soon, the two men were absorbed in conversation.

"My dad is president of the Greenfield Small Business Association," Lucinda said. "He seems to know just about everyone in town. Did you know that he's the one organizing the big citywide fundraiser next week?" Before I could respond, she continued, "The person who sells the most candy bars will get a certificate at my dad's event."

With schoolwork and the newspaper and now Daniel's mystery, I'd forgotten all about the candy bar sales. I was going to have to up my game. I definitely wouldn't win, but I wanted to at least sell a few to help out with the fundraising.

"Are you still topping the leaderboard for our school?" I asked.

"You betcha," Lucinda said. She waved her hand around the park. "I wanted to do something different too. Not the big event, not the fundraiser, but something special that would make an immediate difference." She pointed to my phone to make sure I was making a note of her quote. "This park cleanup was one hundred percent my idea."

"It's great," I said, thinking about how the adults had gone to Main Street the day after the storm to board up windows.

"It feels good to help out," Lucinda said.

For the next hour, I followed Lucinda as she went through the park making sure everyone knew what to do and that the trash was getting carted away. Victoria was helping drag broken tree limbs to the sidewalk, where the trash collectors could get them later.

"When I founded Girls with Goals, I told Victoria, and she loved the idea," Lucinda said.

"Who else did you talk to about it?" I asked Lucinda.

"Just Victoria," she said. "She's my best friend." Lucinda went on, "We filled out the required forms for school explaining how Girls with Goals could help in the community, and we got approved to be a club!"

"Who is your teacher liaison?" I asked.

"We're still working on that," Lucinda said. "We left it blank and just explained that we'd get one soon."

"How many people are in the club?" I asked.

"I haven't counted," Lucinda said. We'd been wandering around awhile and were near Grandfather's cooler. "All this work is making me thirsty," she said, looking enviously at the cooler.

We hadn't actually done much work yet, but I reached into the cooler and grabbed cold cans for each of us anyway.

"Cheers," Lucinda said as she popped the top of her soda. We toasted to the park cleanup with our cans.

I was about to ask Lucinda again about who else was in Girls with Goals, but before I could say anything, there was a commotion on the other side of the park.

"Gotta run," Lucinda said. "Looks like we're running low on trash bags!" She turned to me. "Call me if you need anything else, Jessie. This was fun." With a hop forward, she began to run across the park.

I closed the notes app on my phone and went to help Henry and his friends wash off the playground equipment. As I crossed the grass, I noticed how much nicer the park looked now than when I'd first arrived. Girls with Goals was an interesting club that was doing good things. I looked forward to telling Charla about it all later. I wanted to tell her that Lucinda wasn't as bad as she thought. Sure, she was a little full of herself, but overall she seemed like a good person who was trying to help the town. Perhaps we could all be friends?

Maybe, we both could even join Girls with Goals?

० ० ०

I went to have breakfast with Charla on Sunday morning. I couldn't wait to tell her about the Pickhardt Park cleanup. When I'd left the park, it looked amazing. So clean! Someone had even planted new flowers in a flower bed that had been flooded. The article I was writing in my head was going to be great. I'd forgotten to ask Ms. Surovsky if there was room for photos, but I'd taken some anyway. I hoped we could use them.

Charla was waiting for me outside her apartment building when I arrived.

"I have something important to tell you," she said. Today's shirt read "Nerd Is the Word."

"Oh, good," I replied. "I want to tell you about the park cleanup." I'd gotten home late, and after I'd showered I was too tired to do much else besides watch TV with my siblings. "You go first, though."

When I told Charla to go first, I should have known we'd never get back to talking about the park. She launched into a long story about how she'd spent the previous day with Daniel, "investigating."

There was a piece of paper in Charla's hand. I assumed that was part of her story. "Mom took us to her office," Charla said. Her mom was a lawyer and worked in a fancy building near the river. They got lucky and didn't have any storm damage at all in that part of town.

"Is the office open on Saturday?" I asked.

"Of course not," Charla told me. "But she still goes in sometimes. I explained that we wanted to find out who owned the abandoned restaurant. Mom said those records were public, but you had to have access to them." She added, "We went to the law library in her building, where I could research the address."

Charla waved the paper. "I know who owns the

restaurant!" she said. "And I don't think this lady was the one sneaking around in the dark."

"How do you know that?" I asked. My stomach rumbled for breakfast. I tried to think of a way to hustle Charla's story along. We were supposed to be making waffles together.

"She's nearly seventy years old. Did you see the way that person ran when they heard my cell phone ring?"

I considered this and said, "She might still be sneaky. Or she might have sent someone to the building. Does she have kids? Grandkids?"

"None that I can track down," Charla said.

"Young, spry friends?" I asked. The back door didn't seem to have been forced open, and we hadn't seen any broken windowpanes. "Maybe she sent someone there?"

"Ha!" Charla laughed. "After breakfast, you can ask her yourself."

"What are you talking about?" I stared at Charla.

"Daniel's on the way," she said. "And after we feed you, we need you to be our sidekick." She rethought that and said, "Actually, *we'll* be *your* sidekicks."

I didn't understand what she meant. "I think the two of you have been reading too many Hop-Man comics," I said.

"We're going to talk to her," Charla said. "We'll find out if she let someone in, ask about the art and the boxes."

I had managed to avoid being a detective for a whole week. Now, I could see myself getting sucked in. "What do you need me for?" I asked, though I could already sense the answer. Not only did they want me to solve the mystery, but they needed me to investigate it properly.

Just like I expected, Charla said, "Well, it would be weird if Daniel and I just showed up at some lady's house." She grinned. "But if a certain reporter from a certain student newspaper were to come with us, there'd be a good cover story."

I couldn't imagine what the cover story might be, but I was sure Charla and Daniel had figured that part out already. It was getting harder to tell them this wasn't a mystery, and it was nearly impossible to tell my friends I didn't want to help them.

"Okay, I'll come with you," I said at last. "But only if you put chocolate chips in my waffles."

"Done!" Charla said, handing me the piece of paper she had been carrying. It had a name and address on it.

As I looked at the paper, I thought back to our evening investigation at the abandoned restaurant. We had come way too close to getting caught. I couldn't help but wonder what Charla and Daniel had planned this time.

Chapter 8

Clues from the Past

A woman named Betty Pasternak owned the abandoned restaurant. On the way to her house, I convinced myself that even if she couldn't help us figure out who had been in the building, at least I could practice my interviewing skills.

We found her house down by the creek. It was nicely kept and had a lovely garden. We walked along a path of stepping-stones that led onto a small, tidy wooden porch.

Daniel knocked on the door.

"Go away," a voice called from inside.

"But we—" he started.

"GO AWAY!"

Daniel stepped back. "Okay, what's our plan B?"

I hadn't expected to be standing here today at all, so I didn't even have a plan A, let alone a plan B. I took out my reporter's pad and pen. "Mrs. Pasternak?" I called through the door. "My name is Jessie Alden, and I'm with the *Greenfield Gabber*." I hoped she was listening. The house was really quiet. "It's a school newspaper, and I—"

Before I could finish my sentence, a large, black dog came around from the back of the house snarling and baring its teeth. The dog wasn't moving fast, but rather taking his time, as if he knew he'd cornered his prey.

"RUN!" Daniel took off down the porch toward the street. The dog didn't follow. Instead, he kept his eyes pinned on Charla and me. We'd been too slow to recognize the danger and get away. Daniel was now safely a block away, but Charla and I were trapped on the porch.

"What do we do?" Charla whispered to me. "Got any meaty bones in your pockets?"

"Uh, negative," I said, though it wasn't an absurd question. If I were Violet, I'd probably say yes, because she always had treats for Watch. If I were Benny, I'd have had a granola bar or at least some cookie crumbs.

But I was me, and that meant I had a spare pen and nothing else.

The dog barked. I jumped. Charla grabbed my hand.

I stared at the dog, who was now drooling.

"Don't eat us," Charla begged. "Please."

The dog moved forward, and I pulled Charla back against the front door of the house. "Good doggie," I said, though he didn't seem like a good doggie at all. I tried all the training commands that worked with Watch. "Sit. Stay. Down. Shake."

Nothing. The dog stalked closer. His drool dripped onto the patio.

Charla closed her eyes tight and shouted, "Goodbye forever, Jessie Alden!"

Suddenly, a number of things happened at the same time.

Daniel came back waving a cookie and shouting, "Here, doggie!" He was throwing bits of oatmeal cookie toward the dog. "Yummy treat for you."

The dog looked toward Daniel for a heartbeat, then turned back to us. He barked again, and that's when the door behind us opened.

Charla and I tumbled into Mrs. Pasternak's house,

flopping to the floor in a tangled heap of arms and legs.

"Gizmo!" Mrs. Pasternak grabbed the dog by the collar. "Go to your bed."

The dog tucked his tail between his legs and hustled over to a cushion next to a reclining lounge chair. He spun around three times, then plopped down and immediately started snoring.

"Did my puppy scare you?" Mrs. Pasternak asked, pouring us two glasses of water from a pitcher on a nearby table. She handed us the drinks.

Charla answered quickly and honestly. "Yes!"

"Well, good then," Mrs. Pasternak laughed. "That's his job. You'd be surprised at how many people come knocking on this door to sell me stuff I don't want. Money's tight. I don't want to be tempted to buy anything new." She added, "It seems like everyone in Greenfield is selling chocolate bars lately. I already bought a couple. It's for a good cause, but I can't afford to buy any more."

"I won't try to sell you any chocolate," I promised.

"Knock, knock." Daniel was at the door. He had his hand raised, though he wasn't actually knocking. Just pretending as always.

"Come in," Mrs. Pasternak said, filling a third water glass. "Unless you're here to sell me something. In that case, go away."

"I'm not selling anything. Not today anyway," Daniel joked, looking around the room and spotting Gizmo asleep on his bed. "Is the coast clear?"

Mrs. Pasternak said, "The guard dog is taking a nap."

Daniel still looked uncertain as he stepped fully into the house.

Charla took a long sip of water, and we all calmed down.

I asked, "What made you change your mind and invite us inside?"

"I heard your friend say your name. So you're Jessie Alden?" she said, lowering her glasses to take a better look at me.

"I am," I said, unsure why my name mattered to her.

"I've known your grandfather almost my whole life," she said. "We went to high school together."

This happened a lot around Greenfield. Everyone knew Grandfather.

Mrs. Pasternak smiled as a memory flooded her. "I haven't seen James in years. When you go home, ask him about the Under the Stars dance. That was the big town fundraiser after the last big storm." She stood up a little straighter, and the years seemed to melt away from her wrinkled forehead. "I was his date."

"Date?" It was impossible for me to imagine Grandfather on a date!

Mrs. Pasternak excused herself for a moment, and when she returned she carried a scrapbook. Its pages were stuffed and overflowing.

"One moment," Mrs. Pasternak said as she flipped through old photographs. She finally found what she was looking for and turned the book toward me.

"Oh my!" Charla gushed. "Is that your grandfather?"

Daniel was looking over my shoulder.

The man in the photo was young—about Henry's age—and the woman on his arm was beautiful. I glanced between Mrs. Pasternak and the young lady in the picture. Now, she had gray hair tied back in a tight bun. In the photo, she had dark hair that hung long in curls, and she looked like she was ready to take on the world, strong and determined.

Grandfather, I'll admit, looked about the same as he did now if I squinted. I'd have recognized him immediately.

Behind the two of them were a crowd of people and

a banner that said "Putting Greenfield Back Together." My eyes were drawn to a guy in the back of the image. He wasn't the focus of the frame, but I couldn't stop staring at the way his head was tipped as if he was watching Mrs. Pasternak and Grandfather carefully. There was something familiar about him.

I pointed him out.

"You have a good eye," Mrs. Pasternak said. "That's my brother. He's been watching out for me his whole life. He's very protective," she said. "I'm lucky to have a brother like that."

"What did you do at the party?" Charla asked.

"We danced the night away. James and I won an award for the best twist." She tapped her heart. "He was quite a wonderful dancer."

I'd danced with Grandfather in the living room many times. He really was wonderful.

"The next morning, we helped the town rebuild." Mrs. Pasternak playfully flexed her bicep. "I'm a good dancer, but I'm even better with a hammer." She took back the scrapbook and closed the cover. "So"—she leaned in toward me—"Jessie Alden, what brings you to my house today?"

Since we had family history, I didn't want to keep up the ruse that I was interviewing her for the school paper, so I introduced my friends and explained the truth. "Daniel's family made a delivery to the restaurant you own. They'd like to know what happened to the artwork after it was delivered." I added, "I'm a reporter for the paper, so I'm used to asking questions. I'm helping."

Mrs. Pasternak looked at Daniel suspiciously. "Why on earth would you deliver anything there?"

"What do you mean?" Daniel asked her. "Someone called my parents and placed an order."

Mrs. Pasternak shook her head. "The restaurant has been closed down for months." She shrugged. "My brother and I tried our hand at starting a fancy Italian place using my mother's family recipes, but it proved to be too difficult for me. I'm not young anymore. I'm not able to work that hard." She shrugged as if it wasn't a big deal. "My brother sold everything except the building and opened a wonderful, brand-new business down the street."

"The restaurant has been closed for months?" I asked.

"That explains the cobwebs," Daniel said, which made Mrs. Pasternak's eyebrows rise.

"Have you been snooping around my building?" she asked, her friendly tone from before starting to slip away.

"I delivered the paintings," Daniel quickly explained. "Then we went back to see if they were still there."

"Were they?" Mrs. Pasternak asked.

"We don't think so," Charla told her. "But there were a lot of boxes inside."

"Boxes? That isn't right," Mrs. Pasternak said. "Let's go to the restaurant. I want to see what you saw."

∘ ∘ ∘

The restaurant wasn't too far to walk, so we went together.

Mrs. Pasternak had the key to the lock on the front door, but she didn't need it. The lock was missing.

"I'll have that replaced immediately," she said, pushing open the door. Inside, we were met with a plume of dust...and an empty room.

"Where are the boxes?" Daniel asked. A shocked expression had taken over his face.

He pulled out his phone, and we all looked at the photo again. I noticed that there were squares on the floor where the boxes had been. The dust had settled around them. There were also wheeled tracks leading to the back door.

When I pointed all this out, Mrs. Pasternak said, "Those markings are probably left over from when we moved the last of the supplies out of here." She shook her head. "I'll get that lock changed, but otherwise, nothing here seems unusual to me."

Charla and Daniel were both frowning.

The art was gone. The boxes were gone. And Mrs. Pasternak, the woman who owned the building, wasn't worried about any of it.

Just as I was starting to get as curious about all this as Charla and Daniel were, the investigation had run straight into a dead end.

Chapter 9

Hidden No More

Daniel was waiting by the door of the art room on Monday morning. "Mrs. Pasternak is hiding something," he said as Charla and I approached. "I can't stop thinking about how she was acting all nice to us but also had that scary dog. Then she pretended she didn't know what was happening in her own building."

"Good morning to you too," I said with the smile. "Seriously though, she explained the dog, and I don't think she was pretending not to know about the building. She seemed concerned that the lock had been broken, but when she looked around, she didn't see anything strange."

"But we *know* something strange happened," Charla said as we took our seats. "And she didn't seem concerned to me. More casual about it all." She imitated Mrs. Pasternak. "I'll get a lock. La, la, la. Okay, bye."

Charla was not as good an actor as Daniel. That was for sure. Today her shirt said "I Don't Byte."

"She's exactly the kind of woman who might use checks instead of an app to pay for things," Daniel pointed out.

That didn't sway me. "I really don't think Mrs. Pasternak was behind this," I said. "Didn't you say it was a man's voice that picked up when you called the number at the restaurant?" Before Daniel had a chance to respond, the bell rang and class began.

Groups were working together today, so we gathered at the back of the room. As long as we were clearly making progress on our mural, we could discuss what had happened at the restaurant.

Daniel got out some zebra sketches he'd done and Charla looked them over. I could see our teacher watching.

"What if someone *accidentally* wrote the bad check?"

I whispered. "They'll call your parents for sure once they realize their mistake."

"Yeah, and zebras can fly," Daniel replied, quickly sketching wings onto one of his drawings.

"Nice!" Charla complimented. "I hereby dub him Super-Zebra, Striped Guardian of the Skies."

Daniel quickly began drawing a *SZ* logo on a zebra-size shield.

"I think we've gotten a little too far outside of the project requirements," I said, steering my attention back to the mural. "Forget the check for a minute. What do you each like about zebras?" I'd asked them that question before and they hadn't really answered it.

"I like stripes," Charla said.

"Me too," Daniel put in.

I'd been hoping for a little more to go on, but stripes were where we were going to start. I was thinking about the importance of stripes for camouflage. Maybe we could use that in our poster. Like a hide-and-seek kind of game where we hid zebras in a bigger illustration of the Serengeti or even a zoo? That would be good for the habitat part of the assignment.

I looked over to see Daniel and Charla totally

engaged in designing Super-Zebra's costume. I wondered how I was going to convince them that our zebras probably needed to be more realistic if we wanted a good grade.

"Class." Mr. Masoud stood at the front of the room. "Attention, please." He had set out a wooden easel. It held something that was hidden under a cloth.

"I know you have been working hard on your projects for the last several days," Mr. Masoud said. "I wanted to give you an example of what a creative animal project might look like. I'd prefer if you didn't make a polar bear in a snowstorm." He chuckled as the class realized that would be an all-white painting.

When no one else laughed, he cleared his throat. "I found this piece online—made by a local artist," he said, reaching for the sheet. "The painting shows a unique use of color and abstraction. You'll immediately notice that it's hard to even determine what animal is represented, but as you study the work, you'll see…" He whipped off the sheet, revealing a muddy green canvas with huge brown hexagons. "The habitat doesn't have to be specifically defined."

I was disappointed. There was no realistic animal

depicted, and I felt like this strange painting made Charla and Daniel's comic book character seem like fine art. It was weird. Unidentifiable.

"How is that an animal?" I leaned over and asked Charla.

Daniel muttered, "It's a turtle."

I'd almost forgotten his in-class persona was so shy and quiet. I was getting used to hanging out with Daniel outside school.

"Are you sure? A turtle?" Charla asked Daniel in full voice.

"Correct!" Mr. Masoud beelined across the room toward our group. "Good work! How did you recognize it?"

"I didn't," Charla admitted. "Daniel did."

I looked at Daniel. All the color had drained from his face.

"Tell us the clues that led you to the correct answer," Mr. Masoud said.

Daniel didn't reply. He just stared at his shoes.

I figured I'd help him out. "The muddy green is the main color of a turtle shell," I said. Now that Daniel had identified the animal, it was easy to see. "The hexagons are the designs on the shell."

93

"Good, Jessie." Mr. Masoud began to explain how a good artist can see detail close up as well as seeing the whole thing from afar. "This artist chose a magnified view of the shell."

I couldn't take credit for the discovery. "I only saw it after Daniel said what animal was represented."

Our teacher then focused in on Daniel. "Looks like you win the day. How exactly did you know what this artist was representing in the work?"

"I recognize the artist," Daniel said at last in a voice so soft the entire classroom went silent in order to hear him. "I know his work."

"Very exciting! It's important as an artist to study the works of other creators." Mr. Masoud finished class by encouraging us all to be as inventive as possible with our projects, then dismissed us all.

Daniel hadn't moved from his desk, and he was still so pale that he could have been mistaken for a polar bear in a snowstorm.

Charla looked at him with concern. "Are you okay?" she asked. "You look like you've seen a ghost."

Daniel swallowed hard, then turned toward me and Charla. "You aren't going to believe this," he whispered.

"That's one of the paintings I delivered to Mrs. Pasternak's restaurant."

"What?" Charla gasped in shock.

I had to admit, it was more than a little surprising. How could the painting have ended up in our art classroom?

Charla and I rushed to Mr. Masoud's desk, with Daniel lumbering behind, still shaken.

I explained the situation about the art and the fact that Daniel's family never got paid.

"Oh." Mr. Masoud shook his head. "Do you think the person who sold me the painting online was selling stolen art?"

"Yes," Charla said immediately.

"Yes," Daniel said with a heavy breath.

"Maybe," I said.

"I think I should call the police." Mr. Masoud picked up his cell phone.

"Actually…" I put up a hand. "Is it okay if we ask you to wait a few days?"

"Why would I do that?" Mr. Masoud said. "The website is online right now." He brought up the site on his classroom computer. "Seems prudent to nab the thief while he's still committing crimes."

I could see Charla itching to take a look at the computer.

"We've been asking some questions around town," I said. "We don't want to scare off whoever might be behind the theft. After all, there's still a chance that this was all just a misunderstanding."

Mr. Masoud lifted his beret and scratched his bald head. "Well," he began. "I suppose I can hold off for a little while to see if you can straighten everything out through your investigation."

"I'm not really investi—" I started, but then I realized I actually *was* investigating, and now that we knew this art had appeared online, we really did have a full-blown mystery. The last thing I needed right now was another entry on my to-do list, but I couldn't deny what was going on. "Yes," I said, "Charla, Daniel, and I are investigating the stolen artwork."

I swear Charla and Daniel were holding their arms tightly to their bodies to keep from hugging and high-fiving and screaming, *I told you so!*

"Yeah, we're investigating," Charla said with a chuckle. "So, um, I'm pretty good with computers. Can I check out that website for a minute?"

Our teacher moved aside and let Charla sit in his chair. "I do like watching masters at work," Mr. Masoud said. "Any masters."

Charla's fingers flew over the keys, and before the next bell rang, she told me and Daniel, "Okay, let's go."

"That was it?" Mr. Masoud asked as we started out the door. "Did you solve the mystery?"

"Not yet." Charla looked at me. "Thanks for helping though."

He nodded. "Let me know when I should call the police. I don't want to get swept into something illegal."

"I'll tell you," I promised.

We went out into the hallway. Daniel and I both knew we'd be late to our next class, but we had to know what Charla had discovered on the computer.

"Nothing," she admitted. "I contacted the seller about another piece they had listed."

She described the work and Daniel said, "Yes. That's one of ours too."

"I figured." She explained that it was similar in style: a super-tight close-up of an object. "I used the chat to see if we could meet to take a look at the artwork in person."

My heart began to race. "And?"

"And nothing," she said again. "They said they don't live in the area. If we want the art, we need to leave cash at an assigned spot, and the art will be delivered to us later."

That sounded similar to the way the thief had gotten the stolen paintings in the first place. Only now, the burglar was the one asking for cash. Too bad Daniel's family hadn't demanded the same thing.

"I'm not buying my family's own stolen art from a thief," Daniel scoffed. "That's just silly."

"We aren't buying it," Charla said.

"The fact that they're using a delivery service seems to mean they really are in town after all," I noted while trying desperately to figure out the next thing to do. "If the art was somewhere far away, I'd think money could be sent by an app. Then it would be mailed or shipped."

Charla said, "Just because the seller doesn't want to meet us doesn't mean we can't arrange a meeting ourselves." There was a twinkle in her eye. "Coding club is today, and if I'm piecing this together right, I think I can find out where we need to go."

The bell rang.

"Fingers crossed," Daniel told Charla, winding together his middle and pointer fingers on both hands. Then he said to us both, "Let's meet after Charla is done with coding club. Hopefully by then we'll have the full picture."

Chapter 10

Doughnuts and Dings

We were on a stakeout. It was like when the detectives on TV sit in their car, drinking coffee and eating doughnuts as they wait for the criminals to reveal themselves. Except we were at Jacobs Bistro eating doughnuts and drinking lemonade in a booth. It was a new place that had recently opened, and this was actually my first chance to try it. Even if we didn't get any new evidence on our stakeout, the doughnuts had already made the trip worthwhile.

"What are we looking for?" Daniel asked Charla for the tenth time. He was getting bored. Stakeouts are not as thrilling as they look on TV.

"Whoever sold the art to Mr. Masoud used this café." Charla explained how her coding club teacher had shown her how to track a website's location using something called an IP address. Like with most of her T-shirts, she had to explain what all that meant to me and Daniel. "They were definitely using the Wi-Fi in this café when they posted the artwork for sale online." She let her eyes rove around the room. "That, plus what Jessie said about them using an art delivery service instead of the mail, made me think they probably never left town at all. I'm hoping that it all means they keep coming back to this place to work."

"Right," Daniel said. He glanced around too.

I noticed that one of the building's big glass windows had been broken in the storm, but instead of wood boards securing it like at the art shop, the café had used thick plastic. Light shone through the clear wrapping, creating a dull, foggy glow, and I could feel the wind blowing through gaps in the tape.

Aside from us, there were about ten people using laptops at the café. They hung out at desks, tables, and a few comfy chairs placed at private angles. There were also a few people looking at their phones or their smart watches.

Daniel tapped his toe. "If they are here, how do we find the person that sold the art?"

Charla had to admit that her computer skills didn't stretch that far. She'd gotten us here, but now we needed to look for clues.

"That lady looks nervous," Daniel said, nodding toward a woman who was wearing headphones and tapping her toe.

"She's listening to music," I said.

"That person is blinking their eyes a lot," Daniel said, pointing at a man wearing a bow tie.

"That doesn't mean anything," I replied.

"I'm getting another doughnut," Daniel said, frustrated. He stood up and stretched his legs. "Either of you want anything?"

"I don't want to ruin dinner, but thanks," I told him.

"Same," Charla said.

Daniel wandered off in a zigzag pattern toward the register. I could tell he was checking out any open computer screens and looking for something suspicious, like the website we'd seen.

"So," I whispered once he was out of earshot, "you and Daniel have been becoming good friends lately."

"So have *you* and Daniel," Charla replied.

"I mean"—I glanced over at Daniel, who was now at the counter, pointing at a cruller—"how's your crush?"

"What?" Charla asked as if she hadn't heard me.

"Crush?" I said a little louder after checking that Daniel wasn't heading back our way yet.

"Huh?" Charla squinted at me.

"Remember?" I asked. "When he came to the boxcar, you were all gushing over Daniel's floppy hair. You said he was adorable."

"Oh," Charla said, shaking her head. "Daniel's just a friend. I don't have a crush on anyone right now."

"I didn't know you'd moved on," I said.

"We haven't had a lot of time to talk alone lately," Charla responded.

That was true. We'd skipped last Saturday in the boxcar, and whenever we hung out, Daniel was always with us.

"I don't mind," Charla said, finishing the last bite of her doughnut. "You and me and Daniel: we're like the Three Musketeers."

I knew that those were characters from an old book who had swashbuckling adventures together. Grandfather had told me all about the book and pretty much forced me and my siblings to watch the movie.

Charla recited the Musketeers' slogan: "All for one and one for all!"

I laughed. Our adventures weren't sword fights and chasing bad guys. We'd snuck around an abandoned restaurant, been chased off a patio by a dog, and now we were sitting in a café waiting for something, anything, to happen. But there were three of us, so I guess the motto fit.

"The third musketeer is heading back," I told Charla. Then, looking at Daniel, I added, "But he doesn't have a doughnut with him."

"That's strange, right?" Charla said as Daniel slipped into the booth next to her.

He was out of breath. "I...I...I..."

"Forgot the doughnut?" I finished.

He realized his hands were empty. "Yes...I mean no. I mean..." Daniel caught his breath and explained. "When I went to pay, the register dinged, and I remembered something that I hadn't thought was important."

"When you're looking for clues, everything is important," I said.

"I know that now!" Daniel said. His brain was

skipping all over the place, and he was having trouble telling us what had happened. Daniel kept starting to talk, then looking around the room, then starting all over. "Where was I?"

"The register," Charla reminded him.

It was like light a lightbulb went on in his head. "Exactly! I picked out my doughnut, and as I was getting ready to pay, I heard the register make a ding."

"A ding?" I asked.

"I recognized the sound!" he exclaimed. "Back when I found the piece of paper with the phone number on the counter at the restaurant, I called it and a man picked up."

"The person on the other side said to take the check and leave the art," Charla said, filling in the detail.

"And then there was a ding," Daniel told us. "I heard it in the background before I hung up the phone." He turned and pointed to the cash register. "It was the exact sound that cash register makes. Whoever left me the fake check was definitely here!"

"Looks like we'll be on the stakeout awhile longer," I said. "Now, we have double confirmation that the thief has been hanging out here."

"What thief?" Lucinda asked. She was standing above our table.

I had been so engrossed in Daniel's story that I hadn't seen her enter the café and didn't know how long she'd been standing there.

"I'm working on another story for the paper," I blurted. As I said it, I wondered if maybe I *should* pitch the mystery to Ms. Surovsky. Since a student and a teacher were both victims of the crime, it might make for another interesting feature.

"You'll finish my story first, won't you?" Lucinda asked. I noticed that she gave Charla a strained smile before handing Daniel the doughnut he'd forgotten at the counter. Charla returned it with a blank stare.

"I'm on it," I said. "The park cleanup was terrific."

"Wait until you come to the town fundraiser!" Lucinda gushed. "My dad is going to make this the best event Greenfield has ever seen!" She smiled at me. "I'm still on track to sell the most candy bars, so you can add me getting my certificate to the story, okay?"

"Sure," I said. "If you get the certificate, I'll mention it."

"If?" She laughed. "Oh, you're so funny, Jessie. I'll get the certificate. There's no way I can lose."

Lucinda wandered away.

Daniel noticed the tension between her and Charla immediately.

Charla filled him in on how she had wanted to be part of the Girls with Goals club but Lucinda never called her back. "It's so awkward all the time now," Charla moaned.

"I get it," Daniel said. "Making friends is hard. Without the two of you, I'd probably be at home drawing comics by myself."

"Well, now we're the Three Musketeers," Charla told Daniel.

He grinned. "Oh, let's use that in our art!"

"The mural about zebras?" I asked. I had no idea what he was thinking.

"Exactly," Daniel said. "I've been thinking about the mural ever since class today. I think we can get super creative." There was something about the way he said "super" that made me super nervous.

"Daniel…" I began.

"I'll sketch some ideas later!" he jumped in.

Charla was excited, so I let it drop. It was time to go home anyway, and we could talk about the mural at school the next morning.

On the way out, Daniel noticed the café owner sitting alone at a table, looking over financial records. His head was tilted as he studied the numbers, and there was something familiar about him.

"Hi." Daniel approached the table. Again, I was struck by how different School Daniel was from Not-School Daniel. School Daniel would never just walk up and greet a stranger.

"Hello," the older man replied. He removed his reading glasses and took a long look at the three of us. That's when I remembered where I had seen him before. He was Frank, the man Lucinda's father had been talking to at the park cleanup.

"Are you Mr. Jacobs?" Charla pointed at the sign. "Is this your café?"

"Yes," the man said, pushing aside his work. "Can I help you?"

Daniel dove in, saying, "We've noticed some suspicious internet activity coming from the café."

Mr. Jacobs began to laugh. "How old are you? Are you with some secret government agency?"

I understood his surprise. We were pretty young to be investigating a big art heist.

Charla said, "I've got mad computer skills." She nodded at Daniel. "And he's way into looking for clues." Then she looked at me. "She puts it all together."

"Right," Mr. Jacobs said in a way that meant he didn't really believe we were serious but also wanted to be friendly. "I'll tell you this…all kinds of people come and use the internet here."

"Has anyone ever asked you for help?" I asked. "Like with a website?" It was a long shot, but maybe he'd seen the website and could identify the person we were looking for.

"I'm afraid not." The man chuckled with a hint of sadness. "No one asks me for business advice. This place is barely holding on as it is." He tipped his head toward the broken window. "Plus, I'll admit, I'm not very creative at naming things. Have you seen my doughnut names? Plain with a hole in the middle. Chocolate-covered long ones. Twisted without holes."

"My first doughnut was the round with sprinkles," Daniel said.

"See? Not very clever at all." Mr. Jacobs shrugged. "At least the doughnuts taste delicious." He pointed to his ledger. "As long as everyone here buys coffee and snacks, they can stay and use the internet all day." He raised an eyebrow and asked, "Hey, if I added nicer dinner items, would you and your friends ever come back at night to do homework and eat here?"

"What kind of dinner items?" Charla asked.

"Pizza? Pasta?" he suggested. "Easy stuff that kids like." Mr. Jacobs added, "I've been wanting to expand the business, and I have everything I need to make real meals. We have internet, food, drinks…all we need to be a huge success is more customers."

"Maybe Jessie can write an article about the café for the school newspaper," Daniel suggested. He said to me, "It's nice to help a business grow. You'd be doing a good thing."

"I'll think about it," I said. "Restaurant reviews aren't really my thing." I wondered if the guy doing the cafeteria review might want to extend his beat.

"Let's stay in touch." Mr. Jacobs closed his ledger and stood up. "I've got to go back to the kitchen. Good luck with your cyber investigation." He walked away.

"I think he's making fun of us," I said. It seemed like he was mocking the fact that we were young and investigating a crime.

"Nah." Daniel zipped up his coat as we went outside. "I didn't get that vibe at all. He's just a regular guy trying to figure out how to make his business better."

We both looked at Charla. "What do you think?" I asked her. "Café owner—friend or foe?"

She shrugged. "I'm not taking sides," she said. "When it comes to the three of us, we're all for one and one for all."

Chapter 11

Door-to-Door

Thursday afternoon was the deadline for the first draft of my article on the Girls with Goals club. I had to have a final version in by Monday morning if I wanted it in the next week's paper, so this meeting with Ms. Surovsky was important. She'd give me notes and then I'd work on a revised version of the article. I'd still like to add in a line about Lucinda at Sunday's town fundraiser, assuming she won the sales certificate, but aside from that, I thought I had a really good article ready to share.

"I like where you are going with this," Ms. Surovsky

said as we sat together after school. She spun a red pen between two fingers as she read.

"Great," I said, ready to take notes.

"There's a lot of good information." She pointed out how well organized the park cleanup was and how a lot of people came to help. In the article, I had also mentioned how they didn't have a faculty liaison yet. That was especially interesting because all school clubs were required to have one.

"It's good, but…"

"But?" My heart sank.

"I want you to dig deeper, Jessie," Ms. Surovsky told me. She pointed to the line about the faculty liaison. "Why don't they have a faculty member overseeing them? Have they asked anyone? You should find out. Also, what are the rules about a school club holding an event without any faculty present?"

I hadn't thought that Lucinda might be breaking the rules by organizing the park cleanup without anyone from the school being there. It could be a big problem.

My heart settled, and after that first wave of disappointment, the journalist in me was ready to start fresh, digging into these questions. On the flip side, the friend in me didn't want Lucinda to get in trouble for hosting an event when she shouldn't have—especially because it was a nice, charitable project. But what if Charla had been right about Lucinda all along? What if there was something about her I should be investigating?

I told Ms. Surovsky my thoughts. She said that all journalists have a code of ethics. One of the rules was to make sure I was getting more than one perspective in my story. Another was that I needed to report the truth as best as I could. Finally, I shouldn't get too involved myself.

"I'll do more research," I told my teacher. "Not just about the liaison either." I was going to interview other members of the club and the people at the cleanup. And I even had a few questions for Charla. I wondered if other students had trouble connecting with Lucinda when they wanted to join Girls with Goals.

"I'll look forward to seeing a final draft on Monday morning," Ms. Surovsky said.

There was some time left before club hour ended, and Ms. Surovsky had to meet with other students, so I decided to get started on the revisions right away.

Charla knew where Lucinda lived. She'd been there when she tried to join Girls with Goals and wanted to talk to Lucinda directly. When Charla had gone to see her, Lucinda was of course either not home or hiding in her room.

Charla texted me the address. And then she called. "You'll be at the art shop tonight, right?"

"Yes," I said, noting that it was important enough for her to call me instead of text.

"Promise?" she asked. "We have so much to get done on the mural! After spending so much time on the investigation, we're starting to fall behind schedule on our actual school projects."

Charla was excited about the group project, and I knew she wanted a good grade on it. So did I! But if the newspaper club was going to be my new *thing*, I wanted to give it one hundred percent.

"I know," I replied. "I'll be there."

After confirming the time and promising again, I gathered my things and walked to Lucinda's house. I thought I would start by asking Lucinda who else was in the club.

I knocked. No one answered. I was about to leave when the door opened and Lucinda's dad greeted me. "Jessie, right? How's the article coming along?"

"It's going okay," I said. "I just have a few things to follow up on." I explained about how I needed more sources.

Mr. Dawson was impressed. "You're working hard," he said. "I'm sorry though. I don't know who else is in the club. When Lucinda had needed shirts for the cleanup, she asked me to buy two—one for her and one for Victoria. That way, everyone would know who was in charge," he told me.

I made a note about the T-shirts. It was an odd detail, but I wasn't sure what it meant yet.

"I have an idea. One journalist to another," Mr. Dawson said. "Lucinda has been selling chocolate bars all around the neighborhood." He smiled. "Why not interview a few of the people who bought candy?"

I considered it. Talking to neighbors wasn't going to give me clarity on Girls with Goals, but since Lucinda asked me to write a sentence or two about how many bars she'd sold and had been so adamant she was going to win the certificate for highest sales, I decided it was a good idea.

"Thanks!" I told her dad and headed back onto the street.

I knocked on the door of the house to the right of

Lucinda, figuring that if I was selling in my neighborhood—and not just to Benny—this is where I'd start: the people right next door.

A young man opened the door. He had a baby in his arms and a toddler wrapped around his leg.

"Hi!" I introduced myself and mentioned the article I was writing. "Did Lucinda sell you candy bars for the school fundraiser?" That was my opening question. Once the person confirmed it, I'd ask if she told them about Girls with Goals and what they thought of the charity fundraiser.

"I'm sorry," the man said. "I haven't seen Lucinda in a long time." He called to his partner, then reported, "We didn't buy candy."

Interesting. I went to the house across the street. Certainly they'd bought some candy.

No.

The house to the left?

Nope.

I went up and down the street. No one on the entire block had bought any candy for the school fundraiser. And none of them had heard of Girls with Goals.

Feeling a kind of uncomfortable knot in my belly,

I went back to Lucinda's. Maybe she'd come home while I was wandering around the neighborhood.

She wasn't back yet, but her dad offered to show me her sales sheet. "You can go directly to some of the purchasers," he said. "I'm sure they all have nice things to tell you about Lucinda."

I looked at the paper. Mr. Dawson had bought a few bars. Lucinda's mom too, and another person who must have been family because they had the same last name. Those were the small sales. It wasn't strange for kids to sell candy bars to their family members.

What was strange was the name further down the list. Lucinda had earned her place at the top of the leaderboard and was on track to get the certificate because of one huge transaction. Someone named Juan Barton had bought up cartons and cartons of chocolate. He'd purchased so many candy bars that it only made sense Lucinda believed she was guaranteed the top prize. That number would be hard to beat!

I took a picture of the sales sheet and handed the form back to Lucinda's dad.

"Please tell Lucinda to call me," I said. "I have a few follow-up questions I'd like to ask her."

"Sure thing," he replied.

I left the house feeling like I'd stumbled onto another mystery. Lucinda's behavior with the chocolate sale had definitely been strange. Why hadn't she tried to sell candy to anyone in her neighborhood? And for that matter, why was she still being so secretive about the details of the club? I sighed. For someone who wanted to avoid detective work, I sure seemed to attract a lot of it.

I was headed home when my phone buzzed in my pocket.

"Where are you?!" Charla said before I could even answer.

"Lucinda's street," I told her. "You gave me directions, remember?"

"That was hours ago!"

At first, I didn't understand why Charla was so mad.

"Daniel and I have been waiting for you," she said. "You were supposed to come work on the mural project with us. We really need your help."

I suddenly realized how dark it was outside. I'd completely lost track of time while I was knocking on doors.

"I can come now," I told her.

"The project is due next Monday," I heard Daniel say in the background. "Did you remind her that it's due?"

"You don't have to remind me," I replied. The article and the art were both due on the same day. I had the deadlines in my calendar book. I thought I was on track to get them both done on time, but the night had gotten away from me.

"Forget it," Charla said. "We're going to call it a night. We can talk later."

I opened my mouth to explain everything about how I wanted to make it all work—the project, the mystery, the article—and how I was sorry I had let them down. But before I could get out a single word, the line went dead. Charla had hung up.

Chapter 12

Help Needed

Charla was angry at me. It didn't take someone with impeccable observational skills to see that. She didn't meet me early before school like she usually did, and when I tracked her down at her locker, she told me she didn't have time to chat.

I decided to give her some time to cool off and went back to my own locker to get ready for art class. Lucinda was standing in the hall, so I stopped to talk to her about the candy bar sales. She also told me she was too busy to chat.

I didn't know what to do. I needed both of them to talk to me. And Daniel too.

I headed to class determined to apologize to Charla and Daniel and turn the day around.

"Hi," I greeted them as we broke into our groups.

Neither replied. They hunched over a drawing that I had never seen before. This wasn't the project we had been working on before. First, there were no zebras in it. Second, it looked like a series of comic book panels. Third, I noticed Hop-Man in the middle panel.

"Are we working on the mural design today?" I asked them.

"Daniel and I came up with a different idea," Charla said, "when you were too busy with Lucinda to help us."

"Charla," I said, tamping back my impulse to run away screaming. "I was not too busy with Lucinda." I had an idea to grab their attention. "In fact, I think I stumbled into another mystery."

"You don't want to help solve mysteries," Charla said. "You've made that clear."

"Yeah," Daniel whispered under his breath while studying his drawing.

"Not true," I said, reminding her that I had been all in since that day at the café. "I've been helping with the art mystery all along." I could not believe I was arguing that I was, in fact, a detective! The world felt upside down.

"Whatever," Charla said. She and Daniel put their heads together and started discussing exactly how high Hop-Man could jump and how much higher he would be able to go if he had antigravity sneakers.

"Shouldn't we at least be talking about the mural?" I asked. If I couldn't get her to accept my apology, at least we could finish the project together, right?

"We are," Charla said.

And that was pretty much that. I used the rest of the time to write out a few interesting facts about zebras by myself.

There are three different species of zebras: plains zebras, Grevy's zebras, and mountain zebras.

Zebras thrive in savannahs and grasslands.

A group of zebras is called a dazzle. When the zebras stand together, their stripes "dazzle" predators and protect the herd.

Many zebras can run more than forty miles per hour.

No two zebras look exactly the same. Their stripe patterns are all unique.

When class ended, I handed my list to Charla and asked, "Are we still meeting at the art shop tonight?"

"If you feel like showing up," she said, taking my list without even glancing at it.

"I'll be there," I said, then I hurried off to my next class. I wasn't sure how I was going to do it. I still had to find a way to finish my article, but I knew that if I didn't patch things up with Charla, it would mean big trouble for our friendship. I definitely didn't want her to feel about me the same way she felt about Lucinda.

◦ ◦ ◦

After school, I went home to work on my *Gabber* article. I needed a new way into the story about Girls with Goals and the park cleanup. I hadn't gotten any new information since Ms. Surovsky told me to dig deeper. I was stuck.

And not just stuck on the article but stuck with Charla and Daniel too. I had a couple of hours before I had to go to the art shop. If they were going to act like they had in class, we weren't going to get much done.

I was sitting on the sofa when Violet and Benny came into the room.

"You look sad," Benny said. He handed me some pretzels. "The louder you crunch, the better you'll feel."

I tried it. I discovered that if I stuffed a whole handful of pretzels in my mouth at the same time, the crunching was really loud and echoed in my ears. I noticed that it was a great way to tune out the outside world and focus on my thoughts. Violet preferred one bite at a time. Benny watched us and giggled so hard that he spilled pretzels on the floor.

"What's going on in here?" Henry asked as he entered the room.

"We're crunching away our troubles," Benny said, handing the bowl to Henry.

"How's it going with you, Jessie?" Henry asked, sitting down next to me on the couch.

"It's okay," I told him.

"Just okay?" Violet asked.

I shrugged, then decided to tell my siblings why I was feeling sad.

I told them about writing for the *Gabber* and how my first article wasn't going how I wanted it to. I told them about Charla and Daniel and how I'd let them down on our project. "Everything is due Monday, so there's a lot of pressure. I don't think I can do everything. I'm feeling pulled in a hundred directions, but there's only one me."

I'd been so busy explaining my frustrations that I hadn't noticed Grandfather come into the room.

When I was done, he spoke up. "Think back to when I found all of you." He waved his hand around at us. "I realized that I had made a terrible mistake and missed out on so much of your lives." He leaned over and kissed me on the forehead. "If I could make up for that mistake, then you can make up for a small misunderstanding."

I thought about his words.

"There's always time to set things right," Violet said.

"But everything is due on Monday," I replied, unsure how I could fix it all in two days.

"Solving problems should be done one crunch at a time." Benny smiled. He held a pretzel out to me.

"The kid is a genius." Henry ruffled Benny's hair.

"I get it!" Violet held up a pretzel of her own. "Sometimes it's fun to stuff the whole pretzel in your mouth." She took a tiny bite. "But it's just as yummy to take one little bite at a time."

"I should take little bites?" I asked my family. Sometimes I wished they'd just say what they meant. It took brain power to figure out where this was going.

"Exactly!" they all said together.

Suddenly, I understood. I couldn't write the article, figure out Lucinda's chocolate bar mystery, solve the art heist, get the mural finished, and apologize to my friends all at one time. It would take a lot of little bites to get everything done.

"Know what's better than pretzels?" Benny asked, taking my hand and leading me to the kitchen.

"No, what?" I asked.

"Remember when Daniel brought you *cookies*?" Benny asked, making sure I knew the answer to his question.

"Cookies *are* better than pretzels," I agreed, seeing what he was getting at. "I'll make some and bring them to the art shop," I said, taking out a mixing bowl. "One Daniel and Charla Make-up Cookie Special, coming right up."

"Maybe you could bake a few extra for the brother with the genius idea?" Benny said, licking his lips.

"Of course," I said.

"And one or two for your sister?" Violet asked, coming

into the kitchen and getting milk and butter from the refrigerator.

"I like cookies too," Henry said, grabbing a mixing spoon.

"Did I hear someone say 'cookies'?" Grandfather asked, finding the flour in the cabinet and setting it on the counter.

"We're going to need a bigger bowl," I laughed.

The Alden family got to baking—all of us, together.

Chapter 13

Connecting the Dots

That evening, I arrived at the art shop with a plate of cookies and a prepared speech.

Daniel opened the door. Charla was standing behind him. She'd changed clothes since school, and I liked her new hat. It said "Stuck in a Loop," which I knew meant a section of code that repeated over and over. I'd have complimented it, but I had more important things to say. I launched right into my apology.

"I put my work at the newspaper over my friends," I said, just as I'd practiced with my siblings. "I'm sorry I forgot to come here yesterday. I should have texted when I realized I was going to be late."

Showing respect for someone else's time was important.

"I promised I'd be here, and I forgot." I stretched out my peace offering of chocolate chip oatmeal cookies. "If you'll both forgive me, I'll help you solve the art mystery AND finish the mural."

Daniel took the cookies and studied them. "Uh, Jessie, back at school you told Mr. Masoud you *were* investigating. You're already all in on the mystery."

"Now I am even more all in," I said. "I realized I can help solve this mystery, do the mural, and write for the paper at the same time. I just have to take it one bite— err, I mean, one thing at a time."

Charla and Daniel moved aside and whispered to each other. I waited while they plotted their next move.

After a minute, they came back.

"Okay," Charla said. Then, "Do you want to write words or color pictures?" She and Daniel began walking into the next room, where a large paper mural was laid across Daniel's desk.

"So that's it?" I asked. "I'm forgiven?"

"It was the cookies," Daniel said with a grin. "So delicious."

Charla gave him a playful shove. "We need you," she said. "Two musketeers are no fun."

"We do have one requirement," Daniel told me. "You can't be negative about what we came up with for the project."

I must have made a face because Charla said, "You weren't here last night. Majority rules."

"We decided to go outside the box, like Mr. Masoud suggested," Daniel said.

"How far outside the box?" I asked, feeling a little scared. I wanted a good grade, after all.

Daniel started to chuckle. "Actually, we plan to go inside the box!" He winked at Charla. She full-on belly laughed at their private joke, which made me even more nervous. "We sketched a very rough beginning idea, then stopped because we needed you."

They wouldn't even let me take a small peek until I promised to help them finish the project as they had planned it without being critical.

A promise like that is hard to keep when you don't know what it is you're agreeing to, but I promised anyway. "I'm trusting you both that it's not super weird, like a painting made of pudding or something."

"It's not pudding," Daniel said. "But only because we didn't think of that."

"We could still add pudding," Charla said. "Chocolate or vanilla?"

They seemed to be taking the idea of dessert-based art very seriously. That did not make me feel calm and confident. "Okay," I said at last. "Whatever it is, I'm on board. I'm sure you have a good idea, and I trust you both." These were my best friends. Trust was more important than anything else.

"Close your eyes," Charla said, taking my arm.

"Prepare to be amazed," Daniel said, taking my other arm.

We started across the room when Daniel's mom popped her head in. "Sorry to interrupt," she said. I turned away from the mural and opened my eyes. Mrs. Garza was in the doorway holding an open laptop. "Charla, can you help me with this?"

"Sure," Charla said, though she seemed disappointed that the big reveal of their mural idea would have to wait. We all followed Mrs. Garza back to the front room of the shop.

"I was told that the authorities managed to shut

down the website that was selling our stolen artwork." She put the laptop on her desk and let Charla take a seat.

"Can I check?" Charla asked and Daniel's mom agreed.

Charla's fingers flew over the keys. "Yes, the site's completely gone." She looked to me and Daniel. "Scrubbed off the web without a single trace. Good thing we tracked the website to the café before any of this happened."

Daniel's mom rubbed her forehead. "Now if only we knew who was behind all this. We've filed an insurance claim to see if we can get back some of the money for the art. We've also put in a request with the fundraising committee to see if we can get some of the damage from the storm paid for." She sighed. "This whole situation has turned out to be an even bigger problem for the shop than we thought it would. Not only did we lose a lot of money, but now we have local artists calling us because they're worried about their work being stolen in the same way. If we lose our reputation, other artists won't want to work with us."

I felt bad for the Garzas. They'd worked so hard to build a successful business, and now it was all at risk because someone was selfish enough to take advantage of them. "One of the paintings has already turned up,"

I pointed out. "The others are bound to show up sooner or later."

Mrs. Garza sighed. "I hope you're right," she said. "But on top of that, we still need to repair the storm damage. There are so many people in town that need help. I just don't know if the fundraising will be enough to help everyone."

As Mrs. Garza left the shop, Daniel looked miserable. "I can't help but feel like this is partially my fault," he said. "I never should've left those paintings without anyone being there." A look of determination swept over him. "We gotta solve this mystery," he said to me and Charla. "Getting back the stolen artwork would take a lot of the pressure off my parents."

He and Charla dove in to telling me what they'd discovered about the missing boxes in the abandoned restaurant. "We talked to other businesses on the street," Charla said as Daniel nodded.

"When did you do all this?" I was surprised, especially seeing as they'd made progress on the mural too.

"Yesterday," Daniel said. "You were gone a long time, Jessie."

"Hours," Charla added.

"Sorry," I said again, because I really meant it.

"The thing is," Charla said, moving on, "quite a few other businesses have recently been through the same thing that happened with the art shop."

"Really?" I was impressed that they'd managed to figure out such an important bit of information.

Daniel continued the story. "Around the same time I delivered the artwork, not long before the storm, the toy store, the hardware shop, and the candle collective all had big orders paid with fake checks."

"Were all the boxes delivered to the restaurant too?" I asked. This was an interesting development. I didn't know what it meant yet, but my head was spinning.

"No," Charla said. She rushed to her backpack, and when she returned, she handed me a list of the shops on Main Street. Next to each business, Charla had written the name of the person who had made the order and the date it had been placed. Except for the artwork sale, the other dates were after the storm. That was an interesting detail, but it wasn't really what stood out most to me.

We knew the person who had stolen the artwork from the Garzas had used a made-up name: Johanna

Blart. This was the list of names of who had made fraudulent orders at the other stores:

John Billiards
Jack Boymill
Jae'lynn Breadstone
Janice Brown

"See the pattern?" Daniel asked.

Charla rolled her eyes. "Of course she sees it. This is *Jessie* we're talking about."

"Hmm." I thought about the list of names for a moment. "All these made-up J. B. names sure make it likely that the same person is behind all these crimes."

Daniel frowned. "But that doesn't get us any closer to figuring out who the culprit is," he said.

I wasn't quite sure yet what it all meant either. But I did know one thing: I had seen a similar name pop up very recently, and it was beginning to look like all of the mysteries that had been showing up in my life recently were related.

"Meet me at the boxcar at ten a.m. tomorrow," I told Charla and Daniel. "We're going to use Just Jessie time to track down a thief!"

Chapter 14

A Pattern Uncovered

I realized right after waking up the next morning that with everything that had happened, I still hadn't seen my friends' idea for our art project. We were scheduled to work on it later in the afternoon, after Just Jessie time, so I let the project move to the back of my mind as I focused on the art mystery.

I texted Lucinda to come to the boxcar at 10:00 a.m. too. She got there at the same time as Daniel and Charla.

"Hey," Lucinda said to Daniel and me. She was wearing a new Girls with Goals shirt. This one had gold lettering on a bright red background. Her hair was tied back in red and gold ribbons.

Charla's fluorescent green "Random Number Generator" shirt seemed dull and plain next to Lucinda, which meant Daniel's black sweatshirt and my blue jean overalls were at the bottom of the fashion ladder. If I had to rank us, I fell below Daniel. At least his sweatshirt had a cool yellow swish logo. I looked like I'd been up all night stewing about this mystery and then thrown on clothing from the back of the closet. Which…was the truth.

"Hey, Lucinda," Charla said in a cheery voice. She wasn't going to be ignored anymore and had told me that when I asked if I could invite Lucinda over.

Lucinda glanced at Charla and then blushed. The look confirmed that Charla wasn't invisible. Lucinda could definitely see and hear her.

I hadn't explained to Charla and Daniel what I'd discovered the previous day. I waited until now.

"Lucinda," I began, "Daniel's family had some artwork stolen from their shop." I explained how the art had been ordered and delivered and that the check was no good.

"It turns out that the person who wrote the check didn't even exist," Daniel added.

Lucinda probably hadn't ever heard Daniel speak at school. She seemed surprised at how confident he was here in the boxcar.

"Tell her the name on the check," I told him.

"Johanna Blart." He frowned. "Again, definitely not a real name."

"Your dad showed me your chocolate bar sales sheet," I told Lucinda. "And I noticed something kind of strange that made me think the two things could be connected."

I watched as Lucinda took in what I was saying. At first she blushed. Then she got defensive. "No. No way. I made all of my sales the right way. Juan Barton is a real person. He's a good person. How dare you think otherwise!"

"How do you know?" I asked. "Do you know him?"

"No, but he called on the phone and ordered all the chocolate I could sell," Lucinda said. "He's bringing a check to the fundraiser event tomorrow."

"Juan Barton?" Charla said, eyeing me. "Really? That name sounds just as fake as Johanna Blart."

"I'm going to guess his check won't be any good," Daniel said.

"Hmph." Lucinda frowned. She pointed at me, then Daniel, and finally Charla. "You're just upset you didn't sell as much chocolate as I did. I'm going to get that certificate and my name in the *Goober*."

"*Gabber*," I corrected her again. I reminded Lucinda that my article was about Girls with Goals, not the chocolate sales.

"It's all the same thing," she told me, putting her hands on her hips. "I'm the mastermind behind both. I'm doing so much good in this town that you'll want to put the article on the front page! I bet that will change the principal's mind!" With that, she stomped out of the boxcar.

"Okay. That was weird," Charla said as we watched Lucinda leave.

"The part about the principal was especially odd," Daniel noted. "What did that mean?"

We all shrugged.

"Everything about the whole conversation was odd," I replied. I wasn't sure what to make of it. "Lucinda seemed convinced that Juan Barton exists. Maybe he really does."

"I hope so," I said. "But it's looking more and more unlikely."

Charla fell back into my beanbag chair. "I'm thinking," she announced.

"About?" I prodded.

"Let's say that the person who stole Daniel's art put it online to make money," she started. "Pretend a painting is worth a hundred dollars."

"More," Daniel said. "Way more."

"We're pretending," Charla said. "And you're the best pretender I know, so stick with me here."

Daniel grinned at the compliment. "Okay, fine."

"So the art is worth a hundred dollars. The thief steals it, so it's free to them. They sell it for…" She stalled. We didn't know how much Mr. Masoud paid, so we had to pretend again. "One hundred and fifty dollars."

"That means the thief made a hundred and fifty bucks, right?" Charla said, though she didn't need us to confirm it. She rolled around on the beanbag, hanging her head upside down as she kept thinking. "Five paintings at a hundred and fifty dollars each equals…"

"Seven hundred and fifty dollars," Daniel said.

"That's not too shabby," Charla exclaimed. "And again, it's like free money because the person stole the art to start with."

"Totally illegal," I said. "A person could go to jail for this scam."

"Yeah," Daniel said. "Plus it's mean to steal. They hurt my family business too."

"Right to all that," Charla said, shifting positions again so she was underneath the beanbag with only her head sticking out. "Let's say they stole stuff from the hardware store and the other places, and now they resell all that stuff too, and…" She made up a big number. "Let's say they make another couple thousand dollars."

"The website is gone," I put in. "How are they selling all that other stuff?"

"They get a new site or use a resale app," Charla said. "Not a big deal."

It was a real bummer thinking that our thief might just move on to sell more items somewhere else.

Daniel frowned at that too.

"I'm thinking about chocolate," Charla said. "Seriously, if Juan—or whoever—thinks he can make the same deal as the artwork, order the candy, give her a fake check, steal the chocolate…then what? It's not like he can sell candy on his new website for a million dollars. He won't make much money at all."

"On the flyer, the candy bars only sell for a few dollars each, and the wrappers are marked with the school's name on them in order to track which school sells the most," Daniel said.

"How do you know about the wrapper?" I asked him. We'd been selling on a sign-up sheet. No one had actually seen a candy bar yet.

"While you're working on the newspaper and Charla is coding, where do you think I am?" he asked, rolling his eyes at me. "I'm in a club too."

"You are?" How didn't I know that?

"Mr. Masoud has a few students that come do special art projects," Daniel said. "We work on our own things, but we also designed the candy bar wrappers."

"Did you know?" I asked Charla.

She smiled. Of course she did. Ugh, this was probably another thing I missed out on when I forgot to meet up on Thursday night.

"Who are the other students in the art club?" I asked Daniel.

"Me. Brian Bowman from Charla's coding club comes when he can," he said.

"Brian wants to make animation," Charla said. "Art *and* coding. That's cool, right?"

"And Victoria Kim," Daniel told me.

"Lucinda's friend Victoria?" I asked.

"Yes," Charla said.

"Who do you think is designing the T-shirts for Girls with Goals?" Daniel asked me. "Mr. Masoud arranges the printing after she designs them. Mr. Dawson pays the bill." He added, "I think it's weird she never makes more than a couple of shirts, but her designs are really nice."

He was right. I really liked the red one that Lucinda had been wearing today.

I'd learned something totally new and interesting about Daniel's hobbies, but we had to get back on topic. "About the candy bars," I said, turning back to Charla. "There's no real advantage to stealing them, right?"

"Exactly," she said. "Juan will never make much money reselling those candy bars."

"So why is he ordering them?" I asked her. Then, without waiting for Charla to reply, I proposed an idea myself. "It's not really about the candy bars at all, is it?"

"Could there be another reason Juan bought all that candy from Lucinda?" Daniel asked me.

"I don't know," I said. "But the citywide fundraiser is tomorrow. I have a feeling we'll find out then."

"I hope so," I replied. "Are you two ready to switch gears and work on our project?"

Just like we planned, we headed to the art store. I was looking forward to finally finding out what kind of surprise my friends had for me.

As Daniel opened the door, I closed my eyes and Charla led me to the back room.

"Want to try and guess what it is?" Daniel asked.

"No, I'd rather be totally surprised," I said, letting them lead me to the table.

On the count of three, I opened my eyes.

It was the best idea for a mural idea I'd ever seen! If I had been there when they brainstormed it, I'd have shouted at the top of my lungs, *YES! THAT'S IT!* I couldn't wait to work together to finish the project.

But as excited as I was about our mural, I couldn't shake the feeling that I was still in over my head. We had the perfect plan to finish our art project, but my *Gabber* article was still in shambles, and we still hadn't figured out who the culprit was. As I picked up a paintbrush, I took a deep breath and remembered what I had learned from talking with my family: one thing at a time.

Chapter 15

The Big Day

I arrived at the fundraiser with my family. Daniel was already there with his parents, and Charla's mom had dropped her off on the way to take care of a work emergency.

The event had a 1960s theme and was being held in Pickhardt Park—the same park the Girls with Goals club had helped clean up. Now, there was a tent over the grass and a band playing famous sixties songs. Grandfather knew every word to every tune. A lot of them were from when he was in high school.

After his third lecture about the history of a song, the

band who wrote it, and what Grandfather was doing the first time he ever heard it, I excused myself and went to find my friends. I actually liked hearing about the songs, so it wasn't like I was escaping. It was just that we had a mystery to solve, and I still had an article to write and a mural to finish today, so I was feeling the pressure.

I walked along a row of tables that had a variety of items on display for a silent auction. Many shops in town had donated things to the event. There were candles, books, gift certificates, art lessons from Daniel's parents, hardware, groceries, and so much more. Each item had a sign-up board. If someone wanted to bid, they'd write down their name and how much they were willing to donate. The biggest donation would win.

At the end of the table was a large jar filled with cash. It was for people who wanted to help but didn't want to buy anything at the auction. The jar had a LOT of cash in it. With so many donations coming in, I was hopeful that the fundraiser would be able to help all the businesses in town. Maybe things would turn out okay even if we couldn't solve the mystery surrounding the stolen art.

"Hey." Daniel greeted me next to a table that held

a basket of goodies from the local toy shop. He nodded toward the dance floor, where Charla was letting Grandfather teach her a few classic moves.

Daniel looked ready for the theme party. He was wearing a thin black necktie and a black hat. I had dressed in a tie-dyed shirt, jeans, and sandals.

"They're doing the Watusi," I said, watching Charla and Grandfather. We'd messed around with that one at home over the years. It had been popular with surfers when Grandfather was young. Grandfather spun Charla around, and her woven poncho floated loosely around her shoulders.

I began to ask Daniel if he wanted to go dance too. I could show him that same step. But the way he was looking at the far corner of the tent made me pause.

"What's wrong with Lucinda?" I asked. She still looked as incredible as always. She was wearing a suede jacket that had fringe running all down the sleeves, her hair was pulled back in a braid, and she was wearing a headband, but she looked really upset.

Daniel and I hurried over.

Lucinda was holding her cell phone to her ear as tears started to form in her eyes. We waited a few feet away so we wouldn't interrupt her conversation. As soon as she hung up, she came over.

"You were right," she said, crying.

Daniel took a handkerchief from his pocket and handed it to her. "It's my granddad's," he explained, since carrying a handkerchief was rare these days. "He said it would fit into the theme, but I'm not so sure." Still, it was good that he had one.

"Because of your warning, I told Mr. Barton to bring cash to pay for all the candy bars." She sniffled and wiped her eyes with the handkerchief. "He agreed, but he didn't meet me where he said he would." She added, "And he's not answering the phone."

"Where are the chocolate bars?" I asked, feeling my stomach tighten.

"I dropped them off at a vacant building on the way here," she said. "He said to leave them there and he'd pick them up later."

"You gave him the chocolate without getting the money first?" I asked, trying not to sound like I was judging her.

"Not smart! I know!" Lucinda said, wiping away new tears. "But I trusted Mr. Barton. He was so nice on the phone." She said, "He worked somewhere busy because the cash register kept dinging, so I assumed he was a professional who was buying the candy for a good cause." She blew her nose. "Why would he do this to me? It's awful not to pay!" She bit her bottom lip. "I guess I won't get that certificate after all." She told me, "Please don't mention all this in your article."

I didn't want to make a promise like that, so I just said, "It'll be okay. The chocolate bars weren't worth that much money." That seemed to soothe her for now.

Daniel asked for the address of the place where Lucinda had left the chocolates. Of course, it was the address of Mrs. Pasternak's abandoned Italian restaurant. "Looks like our thief is back at it again," he whispered to me.

And we might have missed our chance to catch the culprit in the act, I added to myself.

Charla walked over. She was sweaty and sipping a cup of water from Jacobs Bistro, which was catering the event. Charla had been dancing and took a minute to let her heart rate lower as Lucinda explained why she was crying. This time, Lucinda didn't ignore Charla, and Charla didn't point it out.

Lucinda needed us to be her friends right now. All of us.

Charla put a hand on Lucinda's back and asked, "What did I miss?"

"I gave away all the chocolate for free!" Lucinda said. "How am I going to explain it to my dad?"

"Tell him the truth. The candy was stolen," I said. "We need to report all this to the police."

"Or solve the mystery and reveal the thief," Charla suggested. "This is just like the situation with the people who placed orders from the town's shops and then gave them fake checks."

"Did you say fake checks?" Lucinda asked.

"Yeah." Daniel told her about the art sale.

"Nothing about any of this makes sense," Lucinda muttered.

"Don't worry, Lucinda," I said, thinking she was still worried about the chocolate bars. "We'll figure it all out."

The band started a drumroll and the crowd fell quiet. Lucinda's dad took a microphone and stepped out onto the dance floor. Everyone stepped back to give him some space to speak.

Mr. Dawson was wearing a deep red velvet lounge

suit. I imagined Lucinda helped him pick it because his socks matched the suit perfectly.

"Welcome!" He circled the floor until he found Lucinda. "First, I want to thank Lucinda and Girls with Goals for cleaning up the park so we could have this event here today." He reached out a hand toward his daughter. "Lucinda," he said, "bring up the members of your club so we can all give them the applause they deserve."

"I—" Lucinda shook her head.

"Let's meet the Girls with Goals!" her dad said again.

Lucinda rushed over to Charla and said quickly, "Come with me! Please."

"Uh, no," Charla said. "I'm not in the club, remember?"

"That's the thing," Lucinda said quickly. "No one is. There is no club. The principal didn't accept my paperwork." She huffed. "No new clubs are allowed until spring semester!"

Well, that explained what she'd said in the boxcar. Lucinda thought that a glowing article in the school paper would turn her luck around and get her club approved.

"Huh?" That was pretty much all Charla could say. She was stunned and struggling for words. "I…huh…what?"

"I'm sorry." Lucinda was talking superfast as her dad

was still trying to get her to come to the microphone. "I'd made such a big deal about starting the club that I was embarrassed to tell you, so I pretended like it had been approved and planned the cleanup event." She sighed. "I made a huge mistake not telling the truth." She added, "I avoided you because I didn't want you to know I was a faker."

This explained why there was no faculty liaison and why Lucinda and Victoria only made two shirts. The shirts made it look like the club was real.

Charla asked, "Was it only me, or did others want to join right away too?"

"Lots of people," Lucinda said. "Since the club wasn't approved, I ignored them all and they gave up pretty fast. You were the most determined."

"Ugh." Charla rolled her eyes.

"Since we'll start over in the spring, you can join the club right now," Lucinda said, glancing at her dad. "Be one of the first new members. It's the perfect time. Let's go." She promised Charla a shirt.

"No thanks," Charla said. "But I'm glad you finally told me the whole truth."

"Lucinda!" Her father was getting impatient.

She looked at me to see if I might want to join the club right now. I shook my head. My article had just taken a pretty big turn. I was going to have to rewrite the whole thing tonight.

"Don't be shy, honey." Her dad held out the microphone toward her. "We're all grateful." He added, "My daughter and her fellow Girls with Goals club members not only cleaned up the park, but Lucinda sold the most chocolate bars for the school fundraiser!"

All around the audience, people began to clap.

"Okay," Lucinda told me. "Time to clean up my mess." She echoed Charla's words. "The whole truth."

Chapter 16

Truth Revealed

Lucinda took the microphone. I could see her hand shaking. "All I wanted was to do something good for the community," she said sadly. "Nothing turned out the way I planned."

I was bouncing between wanting to be Lucinda's friend and wanting to be a good journalist, but then I decided that I could be both. I pulled out my phone and began to record Lucinda's confession. I could decide what went in the article and what I'd leave out later. There was time. I'd make sure everything I wrote was fair and accurate. I might even let Lucinda read it first and give me a comment.

"Did Lucinda and her dad steal the artwork?" Daniel asked me quietly. "It seems like she's about to confess."

"Does that mean they took the other things from the shops?" Charla asked. "All that stuff that was ordered and never paid for?"

"I don't think so," I said. But then again, what did I really know? I started to consider the facts. It didn't take long to realize that I actually knew a lot.

Making a mental list, I quickly ran through what had happened in the past couple of weeks.

Mrs. Pasternak and her brother had owned an Italian restaurant that they decided to close. Just after the storm, someone called Daniel's parents and placed a big artwork order to be delivered to that same restaurant. Daniel got there and no one was around, but when he called the number left on the counter, he heard a man's voice and a dinging sound, like a bell.

In the days after the storm, he heard the same ding again at Jacobs Bistro.

Later, Charla and Daniel discovered a lot of names that had made big orders from local merchants and didn't pay for their deliveries. They all had the initials J. B.

Then Lucinda reported that she'd also heard a ding

when she called the person who ordered all her chocolate bars: Juan Barton. Another J. B.

Suddenly, everything clicked into place. When I figured it all out, I thought I might explode with the answer, but it had to wait. Daniel and Charla were engrossed in listening to Lucinda's declaration.

"A man named Juan Barton placed a huge order for all my chocolates." Lucinda held up her order form. "I was positive that I'd get the highest seller certificate tonight." She didn't take a breath as she continued. "Mr. Barton seemed to really want to help. He even had a lot of ideas for how we could use the fundraiser money to help the town."

She closed her eyes to fight back tears. When she gathered her emotions, Lucinda went on.

"Now I see it was a trick. Because of the chocolate sales, I trusted Mr. Barton. He suggested that I share some of his ideas with my dad, and I did."

Mr. Dawson's eyes went wide in shock. "Lucinda, is this why you kept saying we should make sure the broken windows on Main Street get fixed as soon as possible?"

Lucinda nodded. "It made sense the way he explained

it, but now I can see that he was just using me to try and get his way. Mr. Barton had me drop off the chocolate bars earlier today and then didn't pay for them." She looked at me. "Jessie, can you explain the rest? It's kind of complicated."

The crowd fell silent. I turned off my phone camera and stepped forward.

"Juan Barton is the same person who has been stealing from all of the other local businesses," I said, feeling confident. "He bought art from the Garzas under the name Johanna Blart. He ordered things from all the different shops in town under aliases that had the same initials—J.B." I looked to Lucinda's dad. "It's not Lucinda's fault. She trusted him and thought he was being generous."

"I also thought he'd make me look good," Lucinda admitted.

"I know," I said sympathetically. "But a lot of people in town trusted him too."

Mr. Dawson stepped up to the microphone. "In light of this development, I'm proposing that we expand the scope of our fundraiser. I'd like to use some of the money to pay back all of the businesses that were ripped off by the mysterious man, whoever he is."

"This thief stole a lot of things using a lot of different names," I said. "But I know exactly who Juan Barton really is!"

All eyes in the crowd turned toward me. Charla and Daniel came forward to stand with me and Lucinda.

"Do you really?" Charla asked.

"You and Daniel helped me gather all the clues," I told her. Then to everyone at the event, I announced, "I thought that it wasn't very creative to put the same initials down over and over. It felt like the thief couldn't come up with any other names." I added, "Then earlier this week, I realized the thief admitted to me and Daniel and Charla that they weren't very creative about naming things."

"Aha!" Daniel and Charla gasped at the exact same time.

"The initials!" Daniel said. "I get it now."

Charla smacked her head. "It's soooo obvious!"

"Who is the thief?" Lucinda's dad asked us.

"J. B. is actually—" I began, when a loud voice from the back of the tent shouted, "It's gone. The money is gone!"

Charla, Daniel, and I ran across the dance floor to the auction tables. The auction items were still there, but the cash jar was gone.

Lucinda moaned. "We're too late."

"No. It's not too late!" I told Daniel and Charla, "Get to the Jacobs Bistro tent! The thief is Mrs. Pasternak's brother, Frank Jacobs!" We took off running.

The catering area had shut down during Lucinda's speech. Frank Jacobs wasn't there, but he hadn't gotten away either. We found him behind the tent, packing up his truck. That in itself might have been normal, but there was the cash jar from the auction seat-belted in the passenger seat. He was caught red-handed.

"Frank!" Mrs. Pasternak emerged from the crowd and hurried toward her brother. "Stop!"

I hadn't seen Mrs. Pasternak at the fundraiser, but it made sense that she was there. Jacobs Bistro had suffered damage in the storm too and could use some help rebuilding. She'd come to support her brother, not realizing he'd been stealing from other businesses all along.

"Betty? Betty Jacobs is that you?!" Grandfather stepped up next to Mrs. Pasternak. She'd told us they hadn't seen each other for years. It was an odd time for a reunion.

"Hello, James," Mrs. Pasternak said, looking from Grandfather to her brother. She awkwardly introduced them. "You remember Frank from high school."

"Of course," Grandfather said. "He had a dream to open an Italian restaurant, if I recall."

"We opened it together," Mrs. Pasternak said.

Now, I could see the resemblance from the photo in her scrapbook. I recalled the way his shoulders were in the photo and when we first met him at the café, working on the finance books. He was standing like that, slightly leaning, now.

"The restaurant didn't work out," Frank told the whole crowd standing around his truck.

"I thought we had an agreement," Mrs. Pasternak said. "You sold everything and opened a new business of your own. The bistro is delightful!"

"And I was doing fine," Frank said. "Until the storm hit." He looked at Mr. Dawson. "The flyer for the fundraiser was clear that the businesses that needed money the most would get it first. I only have one big broken window." He sighed, "I didn't think a small shop like mine would get much money at all. It's unfair, but I figured that the bigger, more established businesses would probably get first dibs."

I thought about what Mrs. Garza had said about the art shop getting fundraising money. They didn't think they'd get much help either. It seemed no one really trusted that the fundraiser would help the smaller businesses. For all the good the fundraising was doing, someone had to make sure it was also fair to everyone.

Mr. Jacobs rubbed his eyes as if he had a headache. "The morning after the storm, I decided I would probably have to pay for the damage myself. So I made plans."

"By stealing?" Daniel asked.

"Stealing wasn't my first choice. I hurried to the bank," Mr. Jacobs said. "But they couldn't help me with an emergency loan."

I realized that Mr. Jacobs had been doing his bistro bookkeeping in an old handwritten ledger instead of by computer. I also realized that meant he was the kind of guy to use checks or cash, instead of electronic transfers for bigger financial transactions.

"Why didn't you ask me to sell the old restaurant?" Mrs. Pasternak asked.

"Oh, Betty, that building is yours. You never have enough money for yourself. You can't even buy extra chocolate from the kids. I wouldn't borrow your building money from you." I had to admit Frank *was* protective of his sister, just like Mrs. Pasternak had told us.

I said, "So instead you created a scam to take money from others."

Frank looked down at his feet, too ashamed to answer.

"Oh dear." Mrs. Pasternak was so upset she swayed. Grandfather took her arm to steady her. She looked up at him. "My brother has always been a good person. What happened?"

"Desperation," Mr. Jacobs said. "I didn't have a choice."

I remembered what Grandfather told me. I said, "There's always time to set things right."

The police arrived and arrested Frank Jacobs. Mr. Dawson needed to go to the station to file a report. He said, "Please enjoy the band a little longer. I will make it my personal pledge to try to return all stolen goods and money to the stores that Mr. Jacobs deceived."

The crowd cheered and everyone thanked him.

o o o

Once Frank Jacobs was gone, the band began playing again.

Daniel and I crossed the dance floor and stood by the edge, waiting for Charla.

The song was fun, and I watched Grandfather doing the twist with Mrs. Pasternak. I imagined them dancing together in high school. As they passed by, Grandfather told me, "One more time around the floor, then she'll need to help Frank hire a lawyer. But as long as we have this one song, we're going to make it a dance to remember!" He released Mrs. Pasternak into a spin, and they twisted away.

"Hey, you two want to dance?" Charla joined me and Daniel.

"I don't know," Daniel began. "I wanted to get home early and read the new issue of *Hop-Man*. It's supposed to be a good one, and with everything going on, I haven't had time for it!"

"Oh no!" I gasped, staring at them both. "Are you both leaving me here too?!"

"No way," Charla said, taking one of my hands and one of Daniel's so we formed a circle. "Some things are more important than Hop-Man."

"Hmm…agreed!" Daniel started hopping to the music. "Hop away!" he said as he bounced.

"Hop away!" Charla started jumping too.

I laughed, then I let myself hop up and down to the beat with my friends. Sure, it was silly, but sometimes that's okay. Maybe it was time for me to read my first issue of *Hop-Man*?

Chapter 17

Monday Madness

Mr. Masoud rolled out our mural for the whole class to see. It was the first time anyone had looked at it since we'd finished late the night before.

"My, my," he said, taking in the initial imagery. "It's a comic strip." He called on us to explain.

Daniel didn't want to say anything, but he was willing to stand next to me and Charla. He stared at his shoes while the rest of the class took a good look at our artwork.

I gave Charla a wink. We'd known School Daniel would not want to talk, and we'd planned for it.

Charla began. "Mr. Masoud said that we could be as creative as we wanted."

I added, "Daniel and Charla love comics, but I didn't know very much about them."

"We taught her," Charla said. Daniel nodded, still staring at his feet.

At the top of the of the paper, it said: THE DARING DAZZLERS. That was the name of our comic strip. The three characters were zebras—first, because animals were the assignment, and second, because they were awesome.

Back when Charla was mad at me, one of the facts I'd written down was that groups of zebras are often called dazzlers because their stripes dazzle, or confuse, predators. We thought that was good for our superheroes. One zebra alone might not be able to solve problems, but together they were a team that helped each other.

There were three species of zebras and three of us.

And since another of my facts was that zebras were each unique, we gave them each their own superpower.

The plains zebra could create things out of thin air, just by thinking about what she wanted. For example, she could make an awesome app or a robot that could sell candy bars.

The Grevy's zebra could turn invisible and sneak around without anyone ever talking to him. This allowed him to eavesdrop and spy. Of course, he was the chattiest zebra in the plains, but only when he was with his friends.

The mountain zebra could fly from place to place. She'd always be able to do a lot of things at practically the same time because she could zoom around with superspeed.

In this first episode of our comic, there were three panels.

"In the first panel," I said, "the zebras are at home in the grasslands." This was their habitat and hideout.

"In the second panel," Charla said, "they get a call on the Secret Savannah social network that there is trouble in Greenfield."

"And," I said, "they decide that they are too tired from the hot sun and want to watch videos online instead. So instead of fighting crime, they lay down for a nap."

"Hey," Daniel piped up. "That's not what happens!" His voice was loud, and it echoed around the classroom. Everyone looked surprised. Very few people had ever heard him speak up before.

Daniel looked at me and Charla. We were trying hard not to laugh.

"Okay," he said. "You got me to talk." His face was red, and I thought he might make a break for the exit. Our dazzling zebras could run very fast, and he was about to show the whole class what forty miles an hour looked like as he bolted out the door.

"Finish the story," I whispered.

Daniel looked at me like I was ridiculous.

"Seriously," Charla told him. "Explain the last bit of the story your own way."

Daniel thought about it, then he started. He turned to the artwork and pointed to the three zebras. "The Daring Dazzlers had their first mission. A supervillain was stealing rare gemstones from a jewelry store by pretending to buy them with a fake name." He smiled at me and Charla. "The zebras followed the clues and exposed the criminal," Daniel said with a flourish.

At the top of our mural's final frame, the three zebras were flying off together, ready to face danger and solve the crime.

Daniel fell silent. He'd spoken enough for one day, maybe even for the whole week. Charla and I knew better than to push him further. We all took a bow. Our presentation was done.

The classroom burst into applause.

Mr. Masoud even let out a "Hurrah!"

"What's the next story going to be about?" a boy in the back asked.

I turned to Charla and Daniel. "That's a good question." They grinned at me, so I asked, "Should we work on it together?"

"Yeah," Daniel murmured. "So much yeah."

"This is a wonderful idea," Mr. Masoud said. "We all look forward to hearing what this trio is up to next."

Daniel and Charla and I all went back to our seats, feeling proud.

° ° °

After school, I went to newspaper club. I'd worked hard on the article and left it on Ms. Surovsky's desk before school. Now was the moment of truth.

"Good afternoon, Jessie," she said as I entered the meeting room. My heart raced. Would she like what I'd written? The feature was still about the Girls with Goals club, but it had gone through a lot of changes.

"Sit down," she said, still not hinting at any kind of reaction. She wasn't smiling, but she wasn't frowning either.

"This version of the article certainly does dig deep," she said.

That seemed good, right?

"I was glad that you interviewed the principal about the consequences for Lucinda, since the club was never approved and never had a faculty liaison."

"She is going to do special projects around school," I said. "And she already has a teacher liaison for the spring."

"That's fine reporting. Plus, I love the interview with Charla," Ms. Surovsky added.

Loved! Yay! She loved it!

"I wanted to explore what it felt like to be rejected by the Girls with Goals group," I explained. "And no one felt more rejected than Charla."

"I'm glad Charla was so honest," she said. "Her confusion and frustration reflect in the story."

"I also mentioned that Lucinda apologized and asked Charla to join the new Girls with Goals club." I'd written what happened at the fundraising event and how Charla had refused to pretend she was a member of the group.

Ms. Surovsky still hadn't said she'd print the feature in the newspaper, but now it was clear that she at least liked what I'd written. *Whew.*

"I wish you'd given more information about this bigger mystery around town," she said. "Since Mr. Masoud was swindled, that would have a *Greenfield Gabber* connection as well."

I had thought about dropping the entire Girls with Goals story and writing about the mystery instead, but I felt like I'd committed to the original idea and wanted to stay focused. I defended my decision by saying, "Lucinda's story was important by itself. It's about a girl who wanted to do good but made a mistake. Yes, it overlaps the mystery because of her candy bar sales, but I wanted the reader to see the potential for Girls with Goals to make real change here at school and around town."

"Ah, I see," Ms. Surovsky said. She ran a hand over her hair and pushed up her glasses, then set to reading.

I reached into my book bag and set another article on the table. "I wrote something else for you. This one is about the art theft and the mystery."

After we had finished the mural late the previous night, I hadn't been able sleep. Finally, I'd given up trying and had gone out to the boxcar and spilled my heart into the article that Ms. Surovsky was reading now.

She finished and handed it back to me. "Your feature

on Girls with Goals is good, Jessie." Then she said, "And this mystery article is good too."

I was really happy she liked them both, but my happiness faded when she said, "Choose one."

"What?" I asked.

"Well, there's only room in next week's paper for one article. Which one do you want to print?"

I hadn't thought I would have to pick. They were so different!

I considered that Lucinda was going to restart Girls with Goals, and the article would help with that. But Daniel and Charla had helped solve a big mystery, and the whole town should know what they did.

Both articles were interesting to me. Both articles had important stories to tell.

"Being a journalist is difficult," Ms. Surovsky said. "We think about our subjects, what we care about, what the facts are, and how to present the truth. Then we have to think about our audience and what would impact them the most. Do we want our readers to be happy, sad, inspired, or simply well-informed?"

I was listening to every word.

She went on. "And unfortunately, in a normal

workplace, we usually have to consider sales too. Which stories will get more people to buy the paper?" She breathed a sigh of relief. "Luckily, here at school, we don't have to make that kind of decision because the paper is free to everyone." She asked, "Does that help?"

It did. I considered which was the most important article for the *Greenfield Gabber*. With all Ms. Surovsky's advice in mind, I said, "Please print the article about Girls with Goals."

"Why?" I could tell she really wanted to know my reasons.

"If I am thinking about the subject—Lucinda—I need to present the truth in a meaningful way. I also I think it's the story most connected to students because it's about a school club." I had one last thought. "This is a little against the rule that says I should keep distant from the subject I am writing about, but I think Girls with Goals can make a difference, and I want to help Lucinda get it going again. Maybe if people read the article, they'll sign up." Charla and I had already said we'd participate in her next project.

Ms. Surovsky pushed the mystery article back toward me and took the Girls with Goals feature. "I'll put this one in the paper."

I thought our meeting was over and began to gather my things, but then Ms. Surovsky asked, "Jessie, do you want to be an investigator?"

I paused. More truth. "When I started this year, I didn't think so." After another second, I continued, "But now I realize that I like it. I like thinking through clues and asking questions and putting the puzzle pieces together." I added, "Plus, me and Daniel and Charla are a good team."

She nodded. "That's the subject for next week's feature."

"I don't understand," I said, furrowing my brow.

"Reframe the article." She pointed at the paper in my hand. "Dig deep. Don't just write about the art thief," she suggested. "Write about the detectives."

"I can do that!" I cheered. My heart soared.

"Welcome to the *Greenfield Gabber*." She held out her hand to shake mine. "You are our newest feature writer."

Writer. Detective. Friend. And so much more…

That's me.

JUST JESSIE

(AND CHARLA
AND DANIEL TOO)

10:00 A.M.
TO 12:00 P.M.

EVERY SATURDAY

BREAKING NEWS
There's more to the story...

Follow along as Jessie, Charla, and Daniel continue making headlines!

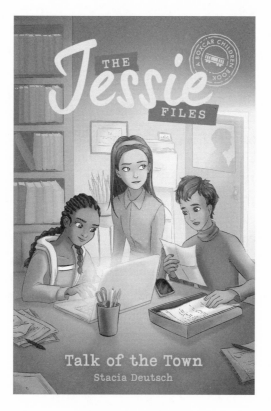

Talk of the Town
978-0-8075-3788-6 • US $17.99
Hardcover available April 2022

Books 3 & 4 coming Fall 2022 and Spring 2023